FNWF 2024 SHORT STORY AWARD WINNERS

GREATER PACIFIC

Paperback ISBN: 978-0-6459322-4-9

First Published in 2024 by

First Nations Writers Festival International Limited T/as First Nations Publishers

A Registered Charity (ABN 79 655 932 979)

2/53 Junction St, Nowra NSW 2540, Australia

Phone: +61 491 851 353

Email: firstnationswritersfestival@gmail.com

Web: www.firstnationswritersfestival.org

FB: www.facebook/firstnationswritersfestival

Cover Design: Busybird Publishing

Typeset: Busybird Publishing

Line Edited: Anna Borzi AM 2024

*Dedicated to all the First Nations
story tellers in the world.*

Your stories create our history, our country,

our customs, our community and our future.

Our hopes, our dreams, our forever after.

Thank you.

Contents

Marlene Dee Gray Potoura

Of Autonomous Region Of Bougainville

The Judges

The Judges said "Simply unimaginable. Simply true. The legends created from facts that protect a culture and its children. Its workers and its mothers. The fertile legends of the Author's culture and soils and natural environment, mythologies and past, are shared with the reader from a deep knowledge. Incredible stories shared."

Marlene dee Gray Potoura's stories are always filled with culture, and informative to read. However, they share deep knowledge of the past and therefore the future. Because we become a people, a community, a nation based on our past. Possibly the most prolific writer in the world, her writing remains of the highest standard. A joy to read. A doyen of literature of the Greater Pacific.

MAUL

Marlene dee Gray Potoura

Prologue

There is no doubt that we inhabit a wondrous, mysterious, and untamed world. People from diverse lands, tribes, and clans across the globe have passed down stories from their ancestors and origins for countless generations.

In the Pacific Islands, we hold a deep belief in the spiritual realm that intertwines with the sea, lakes, and waters; the land, trees, and animals; the air, wind, and gentle breezes; and the fire, smoke, and ashes.

The array of connections is vast, each one cherished and deeply understood within every land, tribe, and clan. As indigenous peoples, our ties to the earth are multifaceted and profound. Nurtured in our traditional beliefs, we are instilled with a reverence for our cultures and taught to decipher the inexplicable through shared narratives and acquired knowledge. We have honed skills and methods to safeguard ourselves from threats that encroach upon our well-being, drawing strength from our collective wisdom and heritage.

I penned this narrative to illuminate the distinctiveness of my homeland, culture, tales, and lineage. I grew up in the Orian valley, nestled beneath the Wukomai mountain, where our forests unfolded like ancient tapestry - a realm where reality and enchantment wove together. The babbling creeks, their voices hushed secrets, held wonders beyond mere water and stone. They were outlets to a magical dimension, where every ripple whispered forgotten tales by our ancestors. Silence was our adversary. To be quiet was to invite the unseen to emerge, a sacred creature, perhaps, or an ethereal entity.

We knew this instinctively, and so we made noise as we roamed through the forest lands. Our laughter echoed among the trees, a chorus of defiance against the unknown.

Yet, there were moments when silence enveloped us; a breath held too long, a rustling leaf, a distant call of a bird. In those suspended seconds, we felt the presence of something ancient, watching. The air thickened, and our skin prickled with anticipation. Was it a guardian spirit, a forest deity, or merely the collective memory of generations past?

Our familiarity with the land was our shield. The forest recognised us - the rhythm of our footsteps, the cadence of our laughter. We were woven into its fabric, part of its living embroidery.

But for a stranger, the forest was a siren, luring them deeper. Their vision blurred, senses heightened, they would stumble toward the edge of cliffs or be drawn inexorably to the water's edge.

And so, we whispered our gratitude to the trees, sang songs to the wind, and left offerings of sacred leaves, unique pebbles and rare vines on ancient stones. For in the Orian valley, we understood that all lands have their wonders, the visible and the hidden, the mundane and the magical. And we knew that our forests, our silent witness, held its secrets close, waiting for only those who dared to listen.

This story is about a man from Simbu, whose name was Maul. He worked for my Uncle Trevor in the early 80s. Before working for Uncle Trevor, Maul worked in Madang for Burns Philp, a group of shops scattered across the Pacific Islands back in the 70s and the 80s. Maul worked in the butchery, chopping up meat sold in the shop's meat section. Maul was a well-built, fearless, muscular man who worked tirelessly.

One of the experiences that Maul first encountered in the coastal areas was the betelnut. He chewed the buai (betelnut, mustard with lime) and loved it. He was thrilled that the coastal people, had this delicacy that they chew, after they eat, or socially, when chatting with friends, acquaintances or merely strangers who came around to enquire for something. He loved the fact that betelnut was meant to be shared and chewed with others, while conversing on the latest news or gossip in one's family, work or neighbourhood.

He had heard from workmates and random buai chewers that Bougainville Island had the tastiest betelnuts and in certain areas, betelnuts were as big as green apples. He longed and dreamt of visiting Bougainville and having the chance of chewing the betelnuts on the Island.

His wish was granted, through Burns Philp because the Burns Philp shop in Kieta, needed an experienced butcher and non-other than Maul was told to shift to Bougainville. He was overly thrilled and excited and in a few days he got on the Air Niugini plane and flew to Aropa Airport. There he was picked up by the company bus and was taken to the single quarters accommodation for Burns Philp workers in Toniva.

Uncle Trevor's house was in Toniva, as he was a private contractor and he owned the land as well as the house. He engaged a lot of Simbu immigrants to work on his cacao plantation in the village. On weekends, he would gather other Simbu friends and they would travel to the village to check on the workers by bringing rice bags, tinned foods, salt, tea, sugar, coffee and other essentials. While he was there, he would walk around the plantation with his friends and admire how cacao plants were thriving.

One of Uncle Trevor's Simbu friend's was a relation of Maul's. So one weekend, Maul had the chance of travelling to the village cacao plantation with Uncle Trevor and his Simbu friends. While there, he chewed a lot of betelnuts and saw the abundance of betelnut trees that grew everywhere and he was flabbergasted at how people had so many trees and yet chew very little of it.

Uncle Trevor was my mother's brother and the land he used to plant his cacao plantation was given to him by my father. So, Uncle was not familiar with the traditional stories that were connected to the land and terrain around Wukomai mountain. My relatives, on my father's side would constantly befriend the redskins (people from PNG) and relate to them in ways and whys they should respect the land, and to be careful not to go to certain areas around the plantation.

Also, they told them stories of creatures, if they see them, they should not kill or harm them. One creature that they should never harm were wolf-like dogs that came around the plantation area in the early hours before dawn. Their appearance and sightings were a sign that someone from our clan was going to die soon. Mostly the pack had a white coloured, two metre in height leader, that has been sighted numerous times throughout the years. Most times they could be heard howling around mountain Wukomai and when the howling continued throughout the week, domesticated dogs would curl up and sleep beside house doors.

The other were pigs with straight bushy tails like dog tails. They were told that if they see these animals wandering around the plantation, they should leave them alone and walk in the other direction.

It is believed that the pigs belonged to the hidden chief and once in a while they would follow him, when he came to our side of the world, because he was from our world. They were also told not to kill any snakes that they encountered while working, as it was forbidden to purposely kill them, if they were not doing any harm but reclining in their habitats.

"We are the intruders. Don't kill them in their own homes," these rules-of-the-land were related as soon as workers came to work on Uncle's plantation. They were told not to go roaming around the terrains of Wuloli, Wukomai and Soro, as these were forbidden lands. "If you cross the line, something will happen to you. If you respect the land and its people, you will be happy here," Uncle told them these words.

After Maul's visit to Uncle Trevor's plantation, he continued to work for Burns Philp. Within a year or so, he was fired from his job so he went to live with his Simbu relation, the one who had taken him to visit Uncle Trevor's plantation a year ago.

During this time, an incident happened with one of Uncle Trevor's plantation work boys. This young man's name was Rarkar and he may have done something, or may have crossed a line somewhere, to make way for what happened to him. Some say, he may have killed a snake while he was working, or may have cut a plant, but what happened to Rarkar only happens when something sacred or forbidden has been destroyed.

One afternoon, Rarkar went down to the Wuloli creek, after clearing grasses around the cacaos, to take a bath for the evening. When he failed to return, his workmates thought he had gone to our house in the village because he was a regular visitor and we enjoyed chatting with him. Uncle Trevor's plantation was an hour's walk from our hamlet.

When he did not show up after three days, two of the workers came to check on him and asked us if we had seen him. When we said no, they told us that he had been missing for three days. Father and mother, went with them to the plantation and they showed them where Rarkar had gone to wash up and since then had not returned.

Father told the workers to return to their plantation house and instructed mother to go and tell my paternal grandmother – his mother – to wait for him in the evening. My father walked through the forest lands, looking for Rarkar. He searched beneath tree trunks, he looked between buttress roots, he peeked in known caves around the Wukomai mountain, he called out Rarkar's name but he was nowhere to be found. He returned in the evening and as he passed through the plantation house on the way to our hamlet, he told the workers to stay in their house until Rarkar was found. He told them to remain calm, as he believed Rarkar was not murdered but was enticed into a different realm, as this was not the first of its kind, he assured Rarkar's friends. He informed them that individuals from neighbouring villages had ventured into our region and had encountered forest inhabitants through alluring or altered states of mind.

Father then went on to our hamlet and talked to his mother. Before the sun was up, my grandmother and her elder brother, my father's uncle, a renowned chief, went to the Wuloli creek were Rarkar was taken and spoke in their old language. After they spoke, grandfather spewed buai and sacred leaves, spoke strange old dialect into the breeze facing the forest lands beside the creek. Then they walked back to the village with the sun rising in the horizon.

One afternoon, as the plantation workers were cooking their meal, Rarkar walked back up the hill from the creek. He was in the forest for about a week. "What happened to you?" his workmates asked as they rushed to his side, reaching out to grab him. He appeared thin and frail, emitting a foul odour, with his eyes deeply sunken into their sockets.

"They took me flying from tree to tree," he replied hoarsely as he collapsed on the ground. He had returned, three days after grandma and her brother had pleaded his case.

My father was summoned for assistance and he drove Rarkar and all the workers to Uncle Trevor's residence in Toniva so that Uncle Trevor could care for them. After a few weeks, young Rarkar recuperated, and the rest of the workers secured new employment, opting not to go back to the plantation.

However, Uncle Trevor found himself in a predicament. With no one left to tend to his cacao plantation, a dilemma loomed before him. Uncle's friend from Simbu, who was aware of Rarkar's ordeal, shared the story with his family.

Maul, who was staying at their home during that period, was intrigued by the narrative. He had a fascination for spirits and forest dwellers, having experienced his own encounter years ago in the highlands while evading the authorities.

He later confided in Uncle Trevor, recounting how he had encountered the mythical creature, Nokondi, during his reckless youth when he was fleeing from the police after being involved in a robbery. He escaped through the rugged mountains of the highlands, and ended up in the Benabena forest lands in Eastern Highlands Province. "Did you truly see the half-man creature?" Uncle Trevor inquired, intrigued by Maul's account, especially since Uncle's mother - my maternal grandmother - hailed from the Eastern Highlands Province.

It was remarkable to hear someone from Simbu confidently affirm that they had witnessed the legendary being, Nokondi. "In reality, Nokondi is not a half-human figure; it is a complete entity that people have only glimpsed partially as it traverses into our realm," Maul confidently explained to Uncle Trevor.

Uncle Trevor, his siblings, and us, their children, were familiar with the legend of the Nokondi, said to inhabit the forests of the Eastern Highlands Province. "The Nokondi is a half-human," my maternal grandmother had previously disclosed. "It is a human with only one half of a body."

Uncle Trevor, intrigued by Maul's assertion that the Nokondi was a complete being and not a half-being, asked him how he came to know this distinction. Maul detailed his experience to Uncle Trevor, recounting how he had hidden and slept nestled between the buttress roots of a tree throughout the night. He had woken up around 4 am and had positioned his chin on the buttress and peered into the mist-shrouded forest floor. As dawn gradually broke through the dense fog, dispelling the darkness, he observed in silence as the misty figures traversed our world.

"The Nokondi can only manifest one side of their bodies in our realm. The other side remains concealed in another dimension," Maul explained. "They exist in the liminal space between two realms, moving between them."

For more than two months, nobody had been working on Uncle's plantation, leaving it untended. There was a pressing need for individuals to maintain the plantation by cutting the grass and pruning the cacao trees whenever unnecessary shoots appeared.

Maul, who was currently unemployed, approached Uncle and expressed his interest in managing and caring for the plantation. Uncle recognised that this man from Simbu possessed unique qualities - he was courageous, physically robust, and at the same time, displayed kindness and respectfulness.

When Maul was relocated to the plantation house, new workers joined, and progress resumed at the plantation, gradually overshadowing the events involving Rarkar, which had now become a tale of the past.

Maul was naturally sociable, he enjoyed engaging with the local community, immersing himself in their language, and assisting them in constructing homes or clearing land for new gardens. His outgoing nature facilitated swift connections with the residents of nearby villages, surpassing expectations.

As a gesture of trust and friendship, my relatives allocated betelnut trees to Maul for harvesting at his convenience. Maul took great pleasure in indulging in the apple-sized betel nuts that he had heard so much about during his time in Madang. The soft, nutty membrane inside, surrounded by a crunchy, moist exterior, emitted a distinct and appealing scent that captivated him. When Maul combined the betelnut with mustard and lime, he experienced a euphoric sensation, feeling as though he had ascended to cloud nine.

Maul's affection for the plantation was evident, and his presence served as a source of strength and inspiration for the workers. Wherever there was apprehension, Maul would confidently lead the way. He became well-known in our village and the neighbouring communities as a betelnut enthusiast, a kind and humble man from Simbu.

The villagers grew fond of him, reciprocating his affection, as Maul demonstrated deep respect for their culture, the women, and the children.

A notable characteristic of Maul was his lack of religious beliefs; he navigated through each day without a specific religious affiliation. Despite this, he consistently demonstrated kindness, diligence, and exceptional caretaking skills at the plantation. Maul found solace in his daily routine of chewing betel nut, enjoying this practice throughout the week.

It so happened that on a fine Sunday morning, Maul and his comrades, went down to Wuloli creek and did their laundry, washed their blackened cooking saucepans, grease stained plates and cups. Then they swam and spent time frolicking in the crystal clear cold creek. At 2 to 3 pm, they climbed up the small hill and walked the short distance to their house. After spending the day at the creek, Maul decided to take a nap on the bench under their house, while his other friends decided to slaughter one of their domesticated hens that roam freely and cooked a nice dinner.

Maul woke up between 4 and 5 pm and he could see the rays of the sunlight passing through the coconut tree near their plantation house. All of a sudden, it started to drizzle, while the last sun rays peeped through the coconut fronds. Just as suddenly as it started, the showers stopped abruptly.

Maul felt a little bit weak because he hadn't chewed any betelnut since yesterday evening, as he was out of betelnut.

He decided to go to the main village and visit his local friends so they would give him some supplies. After informing his workmates of his destination, he retrieved his basket from its perch beside the door.

As Maul strolled along the road that had been smoothed by Uncle Trevor's hired bulldozer to facilitate access to the plantation house; he was struck by a sudden sensation of haziness and heaviness in the air. Pondering whether his longing for betelnuts was compounded by hunger, he found the experience peculiar, given his accustomed routine of working in the plantation without breakfast.

As he lifted his head, he came face to face with a man, who was carrying a large bunch of the best looking betelnuts Maul had seen since he set foot in Bougainville. Maul never saw the old man coming up the road towards him, but the old man may have side tracked from the bushes and came onto the main road, while Maul was keeping his head down. Maul had no idea, but there he was, face to face with a man carrying a bundle of the greenest betelnuts.

"Muleuhu," the old man greeted Maul, as he stopped opposite him. Muleuhu, in the Oria vernacular is a greeting that means 'Good afternoon.' Maul knew that because he had already learned the main Oria language words that he would use to communicate with the older folks. "Aaah muleuhu mani," (Yes, good afternoon, thank you) Maul greeted the old man and stopped beside him to converse a bit and find out if he was selling the betelnuts because Maul had money in his basket.

Now, Maul had never seen the old man before. The old man had the whitest grey hair, on his head and his beard was white and long with a white moustache. His eyebrows and eyelashes were white as well. He had the darkest skin that strangely stood out, reminding Maul of charcoal. He was chewing buai neatly, in his mouth, exactly like all the older folks in the area did.

"Eere irakani lohonke uotoposi," (I am bringing your betelnuts) he spoke in the Oria dialect. Maul just heard, 'irakani' which means betelnut and 'lohonke' which means yours, and knew that the old man was saying that the big bunch of the healthiest greenest betelnuts was for him.

"'O, O, O mani, mani, melahu," (Wow, good, good, thank you) Maul spoke the words rather loudly to emphasise that he was truly thankful. The old man handed the bunch of betelnuts over to Maul, avoiding eye contact and looking down.

Maul got the bunch and admired them closely at how beautiful the green nuts were and what betelnut tree would have produced such a perfect bunch of betelnuts. He turned back to the old man to ask him and there was no one there. Maul looked up and down the road, around the bushes on both sides of the road and there was no one.

He looked at the bunch of betelnuts again and wondered if he truly met an old man or he was just dreaming. Maul did the one thing that saved his life. He carried the bunch of betelnuts and walked on to the village to share with his friends. He did not chew any but continued on to the village.

As he was entering the village, he met my paternal grandmother, the village chief's sister. Maul decided to ask her if there was an old man around the area who grew those types of betelnuts. "An old man, you say, gave you that betelnut bunch?" she asked in her broken tok pisin. "Yes," Maul answered as he went closer to grandma and showed her the bunch of betelnuts.

All grandma did was gesture for Maul to follow her to the village. When they arrived, older folks were called to come and check out the bunch of betelnuts that Maul had brought.

To this day, the story unfolds that Maul was given wild Puriala palm seeds, surprisingly long and large – that made them look like betelnuts, but they are categorised as wild and not edible to humans and in the local dialect would be referred to as 'malangke irrakani' (ghoul betelnuts).

From Maul's description of the old man, the older folk came to the conclusion that Maul had met Ololoupo, the hidden chief of the lands – Wukomai, Wuloli and Soro.

Let's switch over to the tale of Ololoupo. Long, long ago, there was a chief who had two sons. One was a hunter and the other was a fisherman. The fisherman walked miles down to the coastal villages to visit his relatives and they would help him spear the fish with their spears and caught them in their mohuvais (traditional fish net) from the delta and from where the rivers touch and connect to the sea.

From his coastal travels, he met a beautiful woman and brought her to his inland valley village to settle and start a family. The elder brother, the hunter, was enthralled with the forest lands. He would disappear for days and returned with nothing but edible mushrooms. "Why do you bring mushrooms home, instead of wild pigs," he was asked by his younger brother who was married and raising a family.

"The wild pigs belonged to other people. We must raise our own," he told his brother and started bringing piglets from the forests. "You should kill the sow and bring it," he was constantly told and nagged. "I cannot destroy someone else's herd. We must raise our own and stop crossing boundaries to other people's herds," he explained to his people. "I have to politely ask for piglets, so we can raise them," he continued to explain.

He was soon respected in the lands, as a wise man, who was in tune with the forest beings and the one who taught his people to raise pigs in fenced off areas, instead of tramping through forest lands and causing disharmony with careless hunting skills.

He taught his people which wild pigs they should hunt and which ones they shouldn't. He educated them to be aware of the realms that interconnected across the forest lands. He married a woman from his tribe and had children of his own while he continued being the chief of his tribe and lands.

As he continued to rule his people, it became obvious that his disappearance for days into the forest lands, indicated that he was looking after both lands. The land that his people lived on and the land beyond, that his people did not see but respected because of the knowledge he had shared with them throughout the years.

The tale continues that he lived for many years, while his people reached old age and passed on. Stories are told, in different versions that he transcended to the unseen forest land realm, a choice he had to make. And from hence, he still rules his lands. It is believed that he continues to recognize his people and their children's children and at times, he is drawn to strangers, who connect to his lands.

Other times when he'd fail to recognise youngsters who had gone to further their studies and had returned for the holidays, and hung around forests; the young person would be overcome with high fever and vomiting, until old people spoke to the forest lands that he was indeed their own clansman.

So as the generations continue on through the decades and centuries, Ololoupo's tale is told as a legend labelling him as the Sylvan chief of the forest lands. The same forest with its ancient trees has existed through centuries, millennia, witnessing humans and their short-lived lives.

Ololoupo, still continues to emerge into his previous world whenever he wants, whenever he pleases.

"What would have happened to me if I had chewed the betelnuts?" Maul had asked curiously.

"The ancient trees, their gnarled roots, clutching the earth like arthritic fingers, would have beckoned you forward into their realm and you would have followed without hesitation," an elder told him.

"What if I had eaten the betelnuts and had gone into the forest lands but in the end, I would return to the plantation, like Rarkar did," he asked as he continued to make sense of who he encountered.

"Yes, in the past, people have returned, when they were summoned from the other world and were released. But when they entered our world again, they were overcome with insanity, muttering gibberish until they succumbed to their death," an elder explained.

"But Rarkar has healed and is working in Toniva," Maul told the elder.

"Rarkar healed because throughout the week he was somewhere in between the ancient trees; he never ate anything from that world. He returned starving and in need of food and water."

As Maul looked for answers, trying to make sense of his encounter, with what the old people, claimed was Ololoupo, the hidden chief - he was told my story. I was around 15 or 16 years old and in high school, when Maul lived at Uncle Trevor's cacao plantation.

Now, the story that was told to Maul, happened to me when I was around five or six years old. During a certain time of the day, my mother was mending clothes on her sewing machine and I was looking through some pictures from the books in our home library. While doing so, I had fallen asleep and when I woke up, mother was not there. So seeing that no one was at home, I knew that mother had gone to the gardens beneath the Wukomai mountain and I decided to follow her. I walked through my father's cacao plantation and passed by my paternal grandmother who was weeding her kaukau garden and asked her if she had seen my mother. She told me that mother was at Arizona, a land area my father had named Arizona, in remembrance of his best friend Doctor Woods, whom he worked with at Sopas Hospital, in Wabag, Enga Province in the sixties.

As I walked, I started yodelling, "Mamaaaa." Then I heard a reply, "Ooooo." I yodelled again, "Mamaaaaaa." I heard a reply, "Oooooooo." And I followed the sound of where my mother's voice was coming from. I kept on walking and yodelling and would get the reply from the opposite end of Arizona. I followed the reply and went down the small hill to Wuloli creek. I crossed Wuloli creek and went off into the forest lands of the Wukomai mountain and started calling my mother's name in the forest, drowned out by the babbling creek.

As I started crying and calling out, my hands were grabbed from behind and to this day, I still remember the type of zephyr I felt under the huge trees.

I turned around and saw my mother, followed closely behind by my grandmother. Mother grabbed my hands and pulled me out of the vines and shrubs and carried me across the creek, up the hill to the garden lands, as my grandmother shouted angrily into the forest lands, dictating the history of our tribal clan and ancestors.

When we reached the gardens, mother gave me a cucumber to munch on and I hiccupped the aftermath of my sobs.

"Aaaaha, lopisai, malahe, nnkonna tutuka wuotoupi," my mother repeated in a distressed manner. She was saying that 'My goodness, a forest dweller, was at the brink of enticing my child.'

Grandmother had seen that I was kind of sleepwalking and had therefore followed me, because she saw, from a distance that I had taken a different turn at the junction. When I was asked why I had followed that other road that led to the forest lands, I told them that when I was calling out for mother, her reply was coming from the place I had walked into.

"Who was replying to the young child when she was calling out?" Maul had asked confused and tensed.

"There have been stories for generations, on how small children have disappeared, through incidents like the one that had happened to my grandchild. The child would hear a familiar voice call out to them from the forest lands and when they put their feet onto the land the breeze and the air in the forest would muddle up their senses and then pulled them into places where the family could not find them," grandmother told Maul.

Maul was dumbfounded and asked no further questions. And with someone like Maul, who was a level-headed man, he respected the stories that were told to him.

Maul, continued to work at the plantation and he always socialised with his local friends, chewing buai with them and sharing light moments of laughter and stories.

But once in a while, he would stop at the section on the road, where he once met the legendary Ololoupo, wondering if he would ever experience another encounter again.

The End

Acknowledgements

Thank you First Nations Writers Festival International for choosing 'Maul' to be published in your 2024 short story anthology. Much appreciated.

Romney Tabara

Of Papua New Guinea

The Judges

The Judges said "An unexpected tale from the salty and freshy crocodiles of southern and northern PNG, north Australia / Torres Strait and West Papua. An allegory from ancient times to the present. All knowing. It raises the mind to an empathy of legends myths and structures within the natural world; and how when confronted with challenges from encroaching outsiders the balance is lost. Keen eyed and must read. The lesson is clear. Enchanting, horrific, and universal."

Who knew you could fall in love with a crocodile. A whole family of crocodiles, and whole tribes. The intellectual scale and meaning of this story will stay with you a long time. It is a rare writer who is able to achieve that.

A Tale Of Two Crocodiles

Stori bilong tupela Pukpuk

He had been lying belly up on the beach for nearly twenty-four hours now. There were big flies that swarmed around his body, and the awful stench of his rotting flesh drifted through the air.

We picked up on his scent and swam several kilometres before we arrived at this secluded beach. The dead crocodile was my uncle Roger, he was a tough old croc and one of our biggest, measuring eight metres long, and weighing about a thousand kilograms.

He was one whom I always respected and thought was invincible. In crocodile years he would have been at least fifty years old. He was a veteran from the last Salty and Freshy war some twenty years ago. His nose had two distinct scars and he was missing one big right tooth. But there he was lying with a large hole in his stomach and his intestines sprawled out on the sand.

I glanced around and there to my left and my right were my younger brothers Ricky and Danny. They were still juveniles around fifteen years of age in crocodile years, and they weighed in at around five hundred kilograms each. Ricky and Danny looked like twins, they were inseparable and mischievous but they always had my back. If Ricky started a fight then Danny would finish it or vice versa; 'double trouble' was the name given to them by the other Saltys.

Behind us was Big Joe, he was my older cousin and he was much heavier than the rest of us. He weighed at least a little more than a tonne and was roughly ten metres in length. By human standards he was a monster, and in crocodilian terms he was a giant. Big Joe was our enforcer, no one would dare mess with our crew because of him. Joe was feared and respected by all having once capsized a hunting boat filled with fifteen men. He bit the hunter's arm clean off and dragged him down to the bottom of the sea, whilst the others frantically swam to the shore in fear for their lives. All the Saltys witnessed this in broad day light and were terrified. No one had ever taken on the humans like this before and survived.

As I looked into Big Joe's eyes, his cold stare said it all "We're going to get the Freshys who did this!"

We then sunk back into the sea in unison and swam away. Big Joe was Uncle Roger's protégé, he was hand-picked by Uncle Roger ever since we were little. Uncle Roger taught him how to stalk prey, hunt and how to fight. Uncle Roger even took Joe on several hunting expeditions.

My name is Bradley and I am a young adult crocodile about twenty-two years old in crocodile years. I am a saltwater crocodile, a 'Salty'. I weigh about eight hundred kilograms and I am about six metres long, and this is a story about me and my crew.

We live by the mangroves just off the coast of a village called Dawan on the Papua New Guinea side which is a short swim for crocodiles, or for humans a forty minute boat ride from the provincial town of Daru.

For generations we Saltys have inhabited the waters from the mouth of the mighty Fly River in Papua New Guinea along the coast to far end of North Queensland in Australia. While, the Freshys inhabit the rivers from the Middle of the Fly all the way up through its curve into West Papua in Indonesia and its joining of the mighty Sepik River in far Northern region of Papua New Guinea.

The people that lived along the coast were the 'Bala', a resilient lot, tall and lean with dark black skin and long pointy noses. They revered us Saltys as 'Gods'. They once had dances, masks and elaborate ceremonies named after our kind. They studied and learned our ways in their Men's house and named their bravest warriors after us, in the hope that they would join with us in the afterlife.

The Bala inhabited both sides of two very different countries, Saibai in Australia has fine hospitals, schools and shops, including an airstrip and wharf. Even their crocodiles are protected by wildlife rangers making it much safer. Dawan in Papua New Guinea has a rundown school, a small clinic always short on medical supplies, no wharf, no airstrip and no wildlife rangers. Out here we crocodiles were at the mercy of fearful or angry villagers, and local and foreign poachers.

Dawida was now the last remaining man among the Bala who had been initiated in the men's house many years ago.

He had bushy white beard and an afro. He was now deaf and walked around with a long cane stick. He still kept the old ways, and was the keeper of the 'sacred crocodile magic' so everyone feared him and still respected him. It was even said that he could turn into a crocodile at will. No one knew exactly how old he was, but he did recall that he was taught how to read and write in English by the last of the Samoan missionaries brought to Papua by the 'Great Reverend James Chalmers' of the London Missionary Society.

Dawida had seen many changes during his life time, Christianity, education, hospitals and now being replaced with the dangers of alcohol, marijuana, guns and poaching. Gone were the good old days when man and crocodile had a mutual respect for each other.

The new generation were much different. They did not know which parts of the sea belonged to the crocodiles. They no longer travelled in wooden canoes. They now raced through the ocean in faster, louder, bigger and stronger metal canoes that tore through the water with their sharp claws. These new metal canoes were much bigger, stronger and uglier looking, and they even urinated, smelly poisonous liquid into our waters. The people now used their big metal canoes to venture further into our area, stealing more fish in their big nets forcing us to move further from our hunting areas.

I recalled about two years ago, the day that Dawida had passed away and the whole village was in mourning. They were all dressed in black and white and most of them had gone off to church that day to pay their last respects to the late Dawida. The sea was calm and silent but there from somewhere beyond the reef had come in two large ships which had anchored some time the night before. Over the following days this spot became a hive of activity. Several men in frog suits swam around this area, marking it out and taking photos. Then came more men wearing strange yellow hats, they toiled away night and day through wind and rain building a large strange metal platform out in the middle of the ocean. A large metal dragonfly visited the platform every two weeks to drop off men in blue suits who lived on the platform.

Out from the platform came a long sharp beak-like nose which pierced the ocean floor and drew from it rocks and a thick black liquid that lay hidden deep under the ocean. The sounds from the platform sent large ripples through the ocean, scaring away all the fish. The sounds were so high pitched that it pierced our ears, so we kept our distance and watched from the mangroves in horror.

But there was one particular man in a frog suit who constantly checked the mangroves. He came by in his aluminium dingy with a team of five to eight scientists and took photos of us and the other animals. They sometimes laid traps for birds, goannas, fish and us crocodiles. His team tagged us with different coloured pieces of plastic only to come back a few weeks later to check on those of us with the same tags. The scientists also had different gadgets that they placed in the water around where we lived to get readings which they would also come back to check on later.

The frog suit man was always snooping around but in a friendly manner. The man's name was Doctor Eric Sauna and he was an award winning, Environmental Scientist and Author.

He was the founder of a Non-Governmental Organization 'Save the Mangroves' and was doing an environmental assessment on the impacts of mining in the area.

Dr Sauna was a 'Bala' man, he was in his early fifties and was one of the very few to be educated. He was a world-renowned Researcher and Environmental activist having obtained a Doctorate in Philosophy in Environmental Science from the Pierre and Marie Curie University of Paris in France.

Now ironically nearly twenty years later he was now taking on a big French multinational oil mining company to stop them from mining in his home country. Journalists, Academics, Government and the Oil companies clashed ferociously in the newspapers, television, radio and the social media as the local home town hero challenged the big bad oil companies.

Life had now changed for Dr Sauna, he had become somewhat of a celebrity, yet he also now needed armed body guards just to go about his daily business. He was even being talked up as hot candidate to stand for the upcoming election. He even had heavy support from the opposition political parties, businesses and the community. But none of this mattered to us crocodiles, all we wanted to know was, "Where had all the fish gone? Where had all the birds gone? Where had all the deer and pigs gone? What would we eat? Where would we go?" And to top it off we now had a more pressing concern, the possibility of a War with the Freshys.

That night as I nestled at my layer among the muddy wet Mangroves, I kept my ears open to hear elders' special call for a meeting. No one would be hunting tonight, the word had gone out that Roger had been murdered and all Saltys were to standby for the Council of Elders to convene a meeting at 'Birua' the sacred meeting site.

I wrestled with the thoughts in my head that night as I reflected on the images of Uncle Roger's body on the sand. I thought to myself, "How and when did this all begin, our hatred toward the Freshys?"

I recalled when I was a hatchling, the story told to me by mother. My mum was strong and courageous, but most of my brothers' and sisters' never made it out from our nest. I was one of the lucky ones' that managed to survive. You see, life is very tough for a baby crocodile, there were large sneaky Goannas' that lived among the mangroves and they lurked around our nests all day and night. There were even other adult male crocodiles that came around to our nest. But they could not get past my mum, not even one. Our mothers' are very dear to us, we hold them close to our hearts. You see much of what we learn is passed on to us by our mothers and this is the story she had once told me.

"In the time long before the humans when we animals ruled the Land, the Air and the Waters the Saltys and the Freshys lived together. In fact they were actually descended from the brothers Sol and Wara and who were both sons of the Paramount Chief of the Crocodiles,' Papa Pukpuk. But one fateful day they fought over a beautiful young lady, Lewa. A fight to the death was proposed to win the hand of the beautiful Lewa and this fight took place at what is now the Birua, our meeting hall. The fight lasted several hours with both parties battered and bruised but eventually it was Sol who won the fight. But Sol was merciful and spared the life of his brother Wara. Wara was so ashamed of having lost the battle and his honour that he travelled from the Sea up into the river and remained there to this day."

It had now been about twenty years since our tribe the Saltys and our enemies the Freshys had made peace and called an end to the fighting. Since the peace a new more menacing threat had emerged, 'Humans'. These humans had now transformed into creatures of a different world, they had no respect for the laws of nature.

Billy was a young adult Freshy not much older than myself, he was about three meters in length and five hundred kilograms in weight. Billy's home was on the banks of the Gogo River amongst the sago palms.

Sago was the staple food of the Gogo people that lived here in the Middle Fly area. Sago was a starchy powder-like substance obtained from the pith of the sago palm which they baked, fried, boiled and roasted with just about everything they ate. Out here the Gogo people and crocodiles still had a special respect for each other.

Sika was a young Gogo boy about twelve years old from the Waliya tribe. His tribe first came into contact with the outside world in the late 1980's, which was when his parents were born. The discovery of the Waliya tribe on the Gogo River had attracted both positive and negative reviews by the world media. Documentary film crews had frequented the area over the next thirty years making all manner of films documenting the local flora and fauna, to the sorcery and cannibalism practices among the Waliya tribe.

Then in 2020 a special declaration and memorandum of understanding was signed between the Papua New Guinea Conservation and Environment Protection Authority and the

United Nations World Wild Life Fund Program to maintain the wetlands and preserve the endangered wild life that inhabited the area.

Sika often paddled up the river in search of sago. He knew which parts of the river were crocodile infested. He had been taught by his father and grandfather to spot their tracks on the river bank. Then suddenly one day men in orange suits and white hard hats had come in and cleared the sago palms leaving many including Billy homeless.

The only foreign people Sika knew of were the American missionaries from the Summer Institute of Linguistics who were translating the bible into his local language. There was Pastor John Allen, his wife Ms. Debra and their two son's Brett age twelve, and Lewis, age ten. They were from a tribe called Texas in America.

Pastor John was a very tall man, he had soft brown hair and a deep voice. Ms Debra had long soft yellow hair and a lovely smile. Brett loved to play with the village kids and go fishing and hunting with the boys. He sometimes accompanied Sika to go and get sago. Lewis often fell because of the rain and the mosquitoes, so he preferred to stay in the house and push buttons to control the moving people on the big flat box.

Pastor John taught the Waliya about the 'Great Spirit' called 'God' and his son 'Jesus'. Ms Debra taught Sika and the other children how to read and write. Sika's father Kiwali helped Pastor John learn the language of the Waliya. He spent several hours every day talking into a tape recorder for Pastor John. The good Pastor would then play back the recording as Kiwali would listen intently while John typed away on his laptop.

The missionaries had a large house by the edge of the river and Sika loved going there with Brett and Lewis. They would spend hours watching small talking people through the large flat black box while they ate these small mud-coloured bricks that tasted so sweet. It was certainly much tastier than sago or any fruit he had ever tasted before.

Sika was so confused seeing such large groups of men, in strange clothes, all with yellow skin, come in barges all the way up the river and into the creeks. These men did not smile, did not look at all friendly, and they spoke a strange language. They brought with them tools and large machines, they cleared the forests and searched relentlessly through the water looking for strange yellow stones.

The team leader of the mining crew was a yellow skin man called Chan, who was in his late thirties, and had come a long way from his home which was far across the sea. He had left his wife, two boys aged ten and five, and a seven month old baby daughter to come and work for this company in this strange land.

Most of the other workers were also like him from the large crowded cities in his home country. They lived in large concrete and steel structures that were packed with people. These buildings were stacked on top of each other like bee hives.

Chan did not mind as the pay was good and at least he could send money to his wife and family to pay for food, school fees, electricity and clean running water. The miners worked in shifts day and night and they lived on the barge. Sometimes they came ashore to buy food or exchange the tinned food they had for sago, fish and pig meat with the villagers.

The men also, played loud music, smoked, drank alcohol and paid money to lure young teenage local girls onto the barges at night. Billy was equally confused seeing about fifty men for the very first time, with their dishes, shovels and their picks. They threw fire sticks into the creek causing loud explosions, killing fish and chasing us crocodiles far away from them. They dived into the river beds and combed through the pebbles and debris in search of the sacred yellow stones.

Meanwhile that very night further up the river all the way up in the mountain creek of Sapoka, there gathered the Freshys in their thousands at 'Itambu,' the sacred meeting site in the underwater caves. The Sapoka Creek led straight to a series of under-water caves that ran deep under Mount Vosivai at the tail of the Fly River.

The Elder Bubu had sent forth a special cry through the waters, one that had not been heard for nearly twenty years since the truce had been in place. Bubu was a tough old crocodile, he was veteran of the two great Freshy and Salty Wars. He was about eighty years old now and had two missing toes, and a large left tooth. He could not hear or see very well but his battle senses were still as sharp as ever.

Billy listened intently as the Elder Bubu spoke the story again, "In the time long before the humans when we animals ruled the Land, the Air and the Waters. The Freshys and the Saltys lived together in harmony, in fact we were actually descended from the brothers Wara and Sol who were the both sons of the Paramount Chief of the Crocodiles, Papa Pukpuk. But then one fateful day the brothers fought over a beautiful young lady, Lewa. Wara won the fight. But Wara was also merciful and spared the life of his brother Sol, who so ashamed travelled from the river down into the Sea and remained there to this day."

After these formalities, Bubu then went on to give an account of the recent death of an old Salty on the beach. The Freshys were not too sure how he was killed or who was responsible for his death but one thing was for certain the truce with the Saltys was now highly unstable. The Saltys would surely retaliate and all Freshys would now need to be prepared for the possibility of another war.

Billy then decided to flee from what was left of his beloved sago patch. He now had no place to call home and no choice in the matter. Either way he would end up being killed by humans or Saltys. Early the next morning, Billy did the unthinkable, he went against his biological instincts and took to the water whilst most crocodiles were sunbathing during the heat of the day. He swam as fast and as long as he could following the currents down the mighty Fly River all the way to the coast and into the Coral Sea.

Not knowing where he was going or how long it would take. He was now in dangerous territory 'Salty territory' so he stopped intermittently at night at several secluded locations to avoid detection. The salt water was bitter, the ocean currents were stronger than the river currents, his tail was cramped and his feet hurt so badly but he pushed on. Travelling the ocean was like venturing into another world. It was so wide, there were no twists and turns, the fish were bigger and in many different bright colours. In place of logs, reeds and roots, there were colourful coral which teemed with fish and other strange creeping creatures.

Up above there were boats that sped past both day and night. Most rained down cans, empty bottles, plastic bags and sometimes tossed out food. These ocean fish always rushed after these boats as if magnetically attracted to them. The bigger boats tossed out nets, really large ones that dragged everything in its path. Billy was very fortunate and cautious not to get trapped. After nearly three weeks of endless travel through the ocean and scanning the beaches he came across somewhere familiar. Finally, there was fresh water, he could hardly believe it as he ventured forward. The water was warmer, a lot murkier and muddier, there were no twists and turns or under currents. There were tree roots, logs and reeds, fish, yabbies and frogs. It was not as big as the river but it was wide and spacious and definitely not as large as the ocean. But at least the water was fresh and soothing to his skin and scales, and most importantly there were no Saltys, or humans anywhere.

That night the call to war had been sounded as we gathered at 'Birua'. There several large white stones rose suddenly from the deepest ocean like mountains. This place was sacred to both crocodiles and the Bala. Under the rocks Saltys from the deepest reefs to the furthest mangroves gathered in their thousands.

I listened as the elder Lapun gave us several hours of rousing speeches. Lapun was now about eighty in crocodile years he had lived through and fought in two great wars. Although he was old, he still looked tough, he had a few scars on his nose and now had three missing teeth and could not hear or smell very well. He recalled the last great war between the Saltys and the Freshys and the wars before that. He spoke about the great battles and the great heroes, and the casualties on both sides.

We then had a minute silence to remember the late Uncle Roger. Nothing was said about who or which particular Freshy was responsible. No one even bothered to ask if there would be an investigation and who would take the lead. The thought crossed my mind to at least say something about it. But I looked around and there were Ricky and Danny, as dumb as ever with the same blank expressions on their faces'. Big Joe had the same fire in his eyes so I choked back my words and held my peace.

Then after much of the hype had finished it was agreed that we would retaliate against the Freshys for killing Uncle Roger and Big Joe would be the one to lead us.

Early the next morning, I returned to the beach were Uncle Roger had been killed. His body was no longer lying there, nor was his rotting carcass. I looked all around but could not see any sign of his body.

Sniffing around I then picked up on his scent but it had been masked with some other foul smell. I got back into the water and swam several metres down along the beach and there was a small abandoned fishing shack, and an out-door kitchen made of rusty corrugated roofing iron. A large wooden rack was placed adjacent to the kitchen. The smell of strong black tea and smoked fish drifted from the fireplace. Perched on the rack hung the freshly cut skin of a large eight metre long crocodile.

It had been peeled off the animal, and the smell had been doused with salt and some chemical. It gleamed in the bright sun's morning rays.

A White Toyota Land cruiser covered in thick brown mud, with black tinted windows pulled in at the Fishing shack. Out stepped Michael Dwyer or 'Mangi', the New Guinea Tok-Pisin word for 'boy' as he was more commonly known. Michael was about two metres tall, well-built with coffee coloured skin and green eyes, aged in his forties. He was a military man having served for nearly twenty years in the Australian Defence Force, Special Air Services Regiment. He was a decorated soldier having served in Iraq, Afghanistan and Somalia.

Michael's mother was from somewhere in Papua New Guinea. His father was a white man but he never really knew who his father was. He was raised in a Catholic convent by nuns, he had a tough life growing up not knowing where he would fit in. He couldn't call himself "black nor could he call himself white" but in the army he found his true calling. In the army you were not black, white or yellow, in here everybody was made 'green' and he liked it that way. Life outside the army just wasn't the same, he could not fit in no matter how hard he tried. After a failed marriage and two kids who did not want to know him, or have anything to do with him. He decided to go 'walkabout' as the Australian Aborigines call it. A journey that took him from Redfern in Sydney all the way to Saibai Island in the Torres Strait, the place he now called home.

Saibai was isolated from mainland Australia about four kilometres from Papua New Guinea. Supplies came in once or twice a week from Cairns, and sometimes not for a month. But he loved it out here among the Mangrove swamps, giant mosquitoes and black fellas.

Michael was now his own boss, he hunted deer, went fishing and lived off the land. He was primarily a licensed Beche-de-Mer (sea cucumber) exporter, he had a good network with the locals on both sides of the border. He even had his own shed and sorting facility and made some handsome profits when it was in season.

But now there was sea cucumber ban in place and things were really tough. Mangi now resorted to transporting packages through the Torres Strait to Bamaga. He never asked what the packages were nor did he want to know. These runs were carried out in his trusty yahoo dingy 'Bessie' and were made in bad weather and during the dead of the night, or the early hours of the morning.

High rollers in fancy designer suits from Sydney and Melbourne placed the calls, and there was support from all law enforcement on both sides of the border so he just did as he was told and got his cut.

I watched the tall white man from a distance, he wore a cowboy hat, and an old army jacket. On his shoulder hung a double gauge pump action shot gun. He walked around to the back of the vehicle and opened the doors. He then pulled out a heavy black harpoon with a large spear. He pulled out a rag from the back of the car and wiped the fresh blood stains from the sharp tip of the spear. Then he finally pulled out a large net which he dragged on the ground as he made his way to the out-door kitchen.

About a two hundred metres from the shack nestled under the shade of the gum trees was small billabong, a stagnant black dirty pool of water, teaming with mosquitoes and small lobsters. Sniffing through the air Billy picked up the scent of a Salty close by.

Emerging slowly from the water, Billy rested his long nose among the water-lilies.'

In plain sight of the tall man with a shot gun, who then removed from a wooden rack the skin of a large crocodile, rolled it up, and tied it into a bundle before throwing it into the back of his vehicle.

Billy thought to himself, "If we both came from the same ancestor, we eat the same food and even look the same, then why do we now hate each other so much?" He pondered as he sunk under the water lilies.

Out by the beach I decided I had seen enough as I turned to swim away. "Thuddd" I bumped my nose against Big Joe's thick head. He had been floating there quietly the whole time. I looked into his eyes and noticed his pupils grow wider as they began to turn from white to red with rage.

He then blinked, swishing his large heavy tail at the same time. I could now see through his eyes as the image of man began to grow. It was the tall man with pale skin, Joe's gaze went up to the man's cowboy hat, and it was locked there for about thirty seconds. His gaze continued slowly downwards until it met the man's boots where it rested for about a minute before he slowly sunk into the water. I then turned back and took one last look at Uncle Roger's skin hanging on the rack before I too dove into the depths of the sea after Big Joe.

The End

Acknowledgements

I would like to acknowledge the support of my immediate and extended family some of whom are featured as characters in this story. I would also like to acknowledge particularly my mother's people, the Kiwai and Gogodala people of the Western province of Papua New Guinea and the people of the Torres Strait where this story is set.

This story is also a tribute and a testament to the mythologies of the proud river people of the suki, (sago) and sacred crocodile culture of the Western, Gulf and Sepik rivers areas.

I would like to thank First Nations Writers Festival for giving me the opportunity to showcase my writing and I hope to write more books on Papua New Guinean culture to tell our stories to the rest of the world.

Willy Jnr Fafoi

Of Solomon Islands

The Judges

The Judges said, "This story concludes with "People will come and go like the waves hitting the shores of the coastline, but our names will live on forever, strangers will tell our stories, the things we do now will become myths and legends." It starts with myths and legends, and a courageous young woman with a daunting journey before her. Excellent structure, and a story with a lingering memory. Relevant all over the world. All countries. All peoples."

It is so ethereal it could be a dream. Told so vividly, it is as though you are living the journey. The challenges, and the lessons, and the happiness. Immerse yourself.

Lamawa, a girl from Kwai and Ngongosila Island.

Willie Jnr Fafoi

Part 1: The secret garden.

Oh Kwai and Ngongosila, how you lay peacefully, a ray of sunlight reflecting to thy eyes, like a painting in the great sea of Islands, where warriors from past and present rested, a place of peace and comfort, the home above, countries of the few.

These islands are remote and enchanting, known for their vibrant coral reefs, the brave fishermen, and the songs they sing when it's time to sail home.

On one of those islands there lived a girl named Lamawa. She was born to the Ngongosila tribe, a community deeply connected through blood and marriage. These people are seafarers, they hunt, they fish, and they lived by the sea. All their lives and for generations to come, by the sea, Lamawa' s story was passed down and her spirit was as calm and wild as the waves of the ocean.

The journey of Lamawa begins with a secret, a whisper that travelled through time by the wind from stories about a neighbouring island called Kwai. This island, though not too far away, holds many tales of mysteries. There are tales of giants in the Kwai's lush forests, of sparkling waterfalls with goldfish, and the intriguing coconut of youth, where its waters never run dry.

However, no one ever believes these legends, also no one had ever set foot on Kwai's sandy beaches. There was once a man who went there but he never returned, some say he died, some say he regained his youth, so he fears they would accuse him of witchcraft, but still, no one knows what happened to him.

One night during the season of the Lelekoi fish, Lamawa was sitting around the communal fire with her grandmother, Osia, who was known as the wife of the late great chief of Ngongosila. It was a lovely evening, the whole village was sleeping outside on the sand, the Lelekoi fish is said to have a bad omen that would give you bad dreams, so you must sleep outside. It is believed that if you eat the fish and sleep inside your house you will dream about bad spirits.

Lamawa was with her grandmother, and the elderly woman's eyes gazed into the horizon with the wisdom of ages as she began to share a story that would ignite the spark of curiosity in Lamawa's heart.

"Lamawa, my dear," Osia began, her voice so calm and harmonious like a river, "I have a tale for you, a legend that has been passed down through generations." Lamawa turned slowly, her eyes wide with anticipation, moving very close to her grandmother. She loved stories, and tonight's story promised to be about a secret garden.

"In the land of Kwai," Osia continued, "there is said to be a hidden treasure—a secret garden that has been guarded by the spirits of the forest for centuries." Lamawa's heart quickened. "A secret garden, Grandma? What kind of garden is it?"

Osia smiled, her wrinkles deepening like the etchings of time on an ancient tree. "Legend has it that it is a secret garden with a coconut of youth, a sacred gift bestowed upon those who are brave enough to seek it. It is said that the coconut of youth, holds the secrets of knowledge, wisdom, and immortality."

Lamawa's imagination soared like a canoe taking flight on the wind. She had always felt a longing, a desire for knowledge beyond her island's shores. This tale that was told by her grandmother just ignited the fire inside her. "Grandma," Lamawa asked, her voice shuddering with enthusiasm, "do you think I, a woman, is able to take on this task?" Culturally in Malaita province, women are viewed as incapable or limited to certain things, that's why she asked her grandmother.

Osia nodded, her eyes filled with a mixture of love and fear, knowing the village people will not be pleased about this, mostly the warriors of their clan. "My child, you have to keep this just between us, not to mention it to any of your friends. But I believe you are fully capable of embarking on this Journey."

Lamawa, sitting beside the fire, the easterly breeze from the mountain cooling down her face, was lost in that moment. She felt a deep presence of the island of Kwai, as if it were calling out to her, her hands were cold, the smoke from the fire stood still. She knew in her heart that this was her moment, a calling for change for the people of Ngongosila.

With courage and this burning desire, a yearning for afar, Lamawa made a decision that would change the course of history for the two islands. The time has come, the journey has just begun, she would set sail for Kwai, leaving behind everything she had known for something unknown, from a familiar place to an unfamiliar place.

Little did she know that this would be a journey, of challenges, love, and friendship.

Part 2: Journey to Kwai

The Journey to Kwai Island was not an easy one, not the type a seasoned fisherman would take lightly. She spent weeks preparing for her journey, her biggest challenge was to conquer her fear of the sea, so she trained how to sail daily, and the boys in the village started to laugh at her, "what is she up to?", they said.

She gathered supplies, and sought guidance from one of her uncles, Ogafi, the bravest fisherman ever known in the village. Ogafi, despite his initial reservations, without questioning his niece he provides her with all the wisdom of the sea.

Osia, looking at the preparation of her granddaughter, said "remember, Lamawa, the journey to Kwai will be full of challenges, do not lose track or be easily distracted, stay on the path and you will stay alive, the same spirit of Ngongosila that guides me and your grandfather will also guide you, whenever you miss home look to the star to the east you will see me, waiting and cheering for you."

With tears in her eyes and courage in her heart, Lamawa set sail on the dawn from Ngongosila Island.

The small wooden canoe, with space as far as her hands and feet, its bow cutting through the greenish blue waters of the Pacific Ocean. As the island withdrew in the distance, loneliness kicks in, fear, but the excitement of not knowing what is out there is what drives her, a mixture of feelings.

Days turned into weeks, her supplies running low as Lamawa sailed towards Kwai Island. She faced raging seas, fierce storms, and moments when her resolve hesitated. Yet, the desire and the will to reach her destination kept her going, during the night she called on the stars, during the day the wind and sea becomes her guide.

Finally, after what seemed like an eternity and all hope begins to fade away, she spotted the outline of land on the horizon. It was Kwai, the land of the unknown, tropical trees and lush rain forests, waterfalls, and creatures great and small. "Is this a dream or has my imagination taken me far into paradise? am I dead or alive? this place is unreal and never seen before", she said.

She paddled her way to the shore, after two weeks in the sea, her lips had become dry, hands blistered, and she was very tired when she set foot on the sand and the warm sand greeted her feet. The air was thick and fresh with the scent of tropical orchid flowers, and the sounds of the wind hitting the coconut trees, exotic birds singing, filling her ears. She had arrived on the island of Kwai, the land of the coconut of youth.

As Lamawa explored the island, she saw smoke coming from the other end of the island, and she was very hungry and needed some food to eat before she could journey on to the other side of the island.

She collected all kinds of fruit, some pawpaw, bananas, and some sweet coconuts. She then pulls out her fishing line from her canoe and starts fishing. She then baked them and ate until she fell asleep.

She finally woke up in the afternoon at the sound of people talking besides her, "is she dead or still alive?", said Kini, "we should take her to the chief", shouted Siau. Lamawa stood up and said hi to them, and the people of Kwai welcomed her with open arms.

They shared stories of their customs, their reverence for nature, and their own myths about the coconut of youth, and tell her that no one knows the path that leads to the secret garden.

Among them was Kini, a young woman with a spirit as adventurous as Lamawa' s. Kini became Lamawa' s guide and friend. Together, they ventured deep into the heart of Kwai, navigating dense forests and crossing crystal-clear streams. They encountered a strange stream filled with wondrous creatures, that can grant you three wishes only in your time of need, they spend the night there with the creatures and Lamawa asked one of them about the coconut of youth, all that creature ever said was, "follow the sun, the dark night and the half-moon". Then it said to Lamawa, "what are your three wishes", Lamawa reply and said, "lead me in the sun, light me in the dark and give me the moon", the creature smiled and said, "and so it shall be as you wish", they then immersed themselves back into the water and disappeared.

At the break of the first dawn, they began their journey, and it was not without challenges. They were faced with the hottest sun of the day, but were shaded by the coconut trees, encountered the darkest of night, but the mushrooms lit their path, and crossed a swampy lake which because of the lunar, the tide was up so they crossed easily in their rafts.

When they reach the other side of the lake, they realise that all their three wishes have been granted, so they say thank you and continue with their journey.

As they are nearing closer to where the treasure is they hear a very beautiful voice singing, this is a voice so melodious, a sound they have never heard before in their lives. Moving closer they feel the wind on their face, everything was just so still the peace and calmness, time was still, every step they take from there onward is like walking in a dream.

They discovered ancient temples and hidden chambers where the trees were singing, from a distance they saw a coconut standing in the centre of the garden. As they approach the coconut it turned and said, "who dares enter my domain", Lamawa with her head faced down, said, "I am Lamawa of Ngongosila Island, the granddaughter of chief Maela, am here to seek the coconut of youth", the coconut turned and said, "you have come a long way for a curse, how dare you wish to live forever in this perilous world. I remember someone who came seeking this, and after he had lived two lifetimes, he came back and sought for me to remove it. Now he is stuck here with me in an irreversible timeline".

Lamawa looked up to the coconut and said, "I only came here to rescue that man that you are holding, he is my father, in his first life he did not have any children, so when he was about to die he came here seeking you, in his second life he has me as his daughter, all I want is for you to set my father free, forgive his foolishness, that we may go home and never return".

The coconut looked at Lamawa and said, "Ok because of your courage and how far you have come to rescue your father, I will ask you a riddle and you have only one chance to get this right," Lamawa looked at Kini and said, "deal, ask me the

47

riddle", the coconut waved it's branches and said, "how far was the sun in the darkest night when there's a half-moon?", Lamawa quickly remember what the wise creatures have told her, without hesitation she said, " the sun is far in the west, where the mushrooms lights and the tide rises to cross the lake, this is the path to the secret garden", suddenly her father appeared before her and the secret garden disappeared.

Lamawa with a big smile ran and hugged her father, they were both in tears, her father looked at her and said, "I knew you would come for me".

Lamawa's journey on Kwai was an odyssey of self-discovery. She learned not only about the coconut of youth but also about herself. She realised that the true treasure was not just immortality but courage, friendship, and family.

It's these things that holds the greatest treasure of all. In the end, Lamawa and Kini did create a bond, a deep connection to the island of Kwai, which would forever hold a special place in their hearts. Filled with a newfound sense of purpose, she decided to return to Ngongosila Island, not by herself but with her father, not as the same girl but as a warrior and a leader, ready to share her experiences and the lessons she had learned.

Her grandmother was jubilant when Lamawa returned, and she was met with celebration and gratitude from her people. Her father the only remaining bloodline of the chiefdom, the line that was once broken, comes back to life. She became a hero, a beloved storyteller, sharing tales of her adventures on Kwai and the treasures of wisdom she had discovered. Her journey had not only enriched her own life but had also brought a deeper understanding and connection between the Islands of Kwai and Ngongosila.

And so, the legacy of Lamawa, the courageous adventurer, lived on, reminding the people of the Ngongosila that the power of one woman can change the course of history and the spirit of friendship and family were the true treasures of life.

Part 3: Lamawa's Legacy

The return of Lamawa to Ngongosila Island marked the beginning of a union between the two islands. The return of her father the chief brought order back into the community. Lamawa shared some of the knowledge she learned from the people of Kwai with the Ngongosila tribe, and they learn about new fishing techniques, gardening and how to prepare certain type of foods that can be used during the dry season.

The Ngongosila people are fishermen, little did they know about gardening, with this knowledge, they learned new techniques for cultivating crops and building more resilient structures. Also, about traditional medicines, healing properties of herbs and plants previously unknown to them, the use of marijuana as a prayer leaf.

She tells stories of her adventure, the tale about the wise water creatures and the wishes they grant you in your times of need. Lamawa also shared the types of tools and weapons they used, their uses and how they are made. The people of Kwai are environmental loving people, they emphasise more the importance of harmony with nature and the need to protect the forest for the future generations. So, most of their customs and laws always align with nature, under the guidance of Lamawa, she shared this wisdom with the people of Ngongosila Island to embrace sustainable practices, ensuring the preservation of their environment for future generations.

Despite Lamawa's great achievements, her spirit of adventure and exploration will never stop there. She had daily meetings with the youths of the community about dreaming big, to have courage and let nothing hold you back from achieving your goals in life. She becomes a beacon of hope, a symbol of strength and courage for the village youths, an example of someone with nothing can become something. On the first season of the moon fish, when the wind is high, many people were inspired by the stories and tales of Kwai, so some decide to embark on their own journeys of exploration to visit Kwai Island. They set sail to neighbouring Kwai islands, not just in search of knowledge but also to foster connections and friendships with their island neighbours.

The bonds between the communities of the Kwai and Ngongosila grew stronger, and they began to see themselves not as isolated islands but as interconnected parts of a great family.

As the years passed, the route between Kwai and Ngongosila became an economic centre for other neighbouring islands. They develop a buying system where shell money becomes their currency, people trade all sorts of things.

Lamawa, now a woman in the Ngongosila tribe, was very vocal and an important leader in the development of her community, her hair becomes darker with age but her spirit was as vibrant as ever. People all over the islands, heard about her stories, which were cherished by generations, she often told the tale of her journey to Kwai and the how it had transformed her life.

The island of Ngongosila prospered, not only in material wealth but also in the richness of its culture and the depth of its connections with neighbouring islands. The legacy of Lamawa lived on, carried on from Islands to Islands.

Part 4: Lamawa found Love.

Before the passing away of Osia, she called Lamawa beside her bed and said to her, "you have done much now for this community, now its time you do something for yourself, now you are older, you should find someone to marry, this is my last wish for you, my daughter".

Osia passed away at the age of 70 years old, she was a strong woman, someone who loves everyone and has the wisdom of the sea and land. Lamawa was heartbroken, but she found peace.

After all, now there is a new task ahead of her, to find love, to make sure her grandmother's last wish is granted. After the burial of her grandmother, she went out to sea and said her last goodbyes, looking towards Ramos Island, she said her prayers then submerged herself into the sea.

The people of Kwai believe when their ancestors died, their spirits go and lived on the Island of the Ramos.

At the end of every harvest month there will always be a great feast, it is called the "Maoma", this is the time of the year where all the bounty of the harvest will be brought together and all will be sharing the abundance. All kinds of root crops, fruits and special types of food will be prepared. Hunters will go out into the jungle and hunt for wild pigs, fishermen will set sail to the far end of the open reefs for the biggest catch of the year, all the necessary food items that are available will be prepared and brought to the table.

During this event all sorts of games and entertainment will be displayed, there will be singing and dancing. A canoe race, swim race, walking on fire and the best one of all is the eating contest. All the great warriors of the tribe will stand out to show who's the strongest, they would line up in front of the table, with their hands tied behind their backs and start eating, whoever finishes first will be crowned the new reigning champion.

For most of the young men in the village this is one of the opportunities for them to look for the girl of their dream, a time to be the man, to do whatever it takes to attract the ladies that are there to attend the festival. One thing that makes the event more special is, the invitation was also sent to the people of Kwai Island to attend the feast, so they came with everything they have.

Among the delegation from Kwai Island, was Oge, the son of the chief of Kwai, he accompanies his father, Chief Luda to attend the ceremony. They brought with them pigs of all sizes, root crops and some shell money to present as gifts to the Chief of Ngongosila Island.

During the presentation Lamawa saw her old friend Kini, and she runs to her, greeting each other with hugs and tears, "long time no see my sister", Lamawa said to Kini, she replied and said, "they wanted me not to come, but I insisted that I must come to see you".

After the presentation and welcoming ceremony for all the participating tribes, the chief of Ngongosila rose and declared the Maoma is now open. Now all the people came together and start preparing the food, the pigs were slaughtered, all the fish were prepared by the women and all the root crops were taken care-off by the young ladies. After all the food was ready and baked in the oven "*Gwabi*", it' was the time for entertainment.

Each tribe performed one of their sacred dances, the performance going on until daybreak. It is traditional to the people of Malaita that during an entrance dance by the warriors, the women must cover their eyes, to avoid falling under a spell that will make them attracted to the dancers. The dancers were covered with all the traditional costumes, shells on their foreheads, war clubs in their hands, flowers, and decorations all over their bodies, it was a sight to see.

The delegation from Kwai Islands were the fourth group to perform that night. The drums were beating, and the conch shells were screaming, the crowd impatiently shouting whilst the warriors were chanting and about to make an entrance. It was a sight they have never seen before, the dazzling shells, mud paintings, colourful bird feathers, the beauty and culture of Kwai was on full display.

Suddenly the drums stop, and the crowd goes silent, then warriors scream and make their entrance. They were all as one, in harmony and aligned together as they come out to the dancing ground, Oge the chief's son was leading the line, all the women in the crowd were covering their eyes, believing the spell that the dancers coming out with would affect them. The crowd goes so wild during the entrance everybody was on their feet.

When the Kwai dancers begin their second dance song, Lamawa was in the distance, her eyes was just fixed on Oge, his every move was just like a vessel under the radar, monitoring him every step of the way. When Oge lift his eyes, he looks no other way but into Lamawa's eye, just like a Mexican duel, there was no turning back from there. Lamawa's heart was like a spark of fire igniting inside of her, that butterfly tummy feeling flying everywhere inside her. She was smiling and kept talking to herself, "what is this feeling, why am I finding it hard to breath", she said.

After the dance, Oge came and looked for her in the crowd but could not find her, he searches everywhere but could not see her. He then runs up to Kini and said, "did you see Lamawa", Kini look at him and said, "hey be careful you do not want to start trouble for your father", he smiled and said, "the way she looks at me, I know she is the one".

It was at the breaking of the dawn when he looks at the end of the island, beneath a coconut, Lamawa was sitting by herself. He pulls all his courage together and walks towards Lamawa, and she turned and saw this young well-built specimen of a man walking towards her, she smiled, and he smiled back at her. They spend the whole dawn together till the daybreak.

Before the sun reflects on the sea harbour, Lamawa got up and said, I must go back before my father started looking for me. Oge, stood up and said, "how can we see each other again", Lamawa replied, "if you want me, go and ask my father".

The next day, it was a very beautiful morning, everyone was still asleep, the smoke from the fire from the night was still burning. All the women were already up preparing the food for the feast, they were arranging the distribution of food to where the feast is going to happen. The men were at the venue arranging the huts where each tribe will be sitting, all the children were running everywhere, some even start swimming in the sea, all were looking forward for the feast.

With all the commotion and everything happening around, Oge's mind was just fixed on one thing, that is to go and ask for Lamawa's hand for marriage. He went to the hut where all the chiefs were residing and asked to see his father.

His father came out from the hut and ask him what's the trouble. He looked to his father and said, "Father, I want to ask for Lamawa's hand in marriage and I want you to talk to her father about it", his father look at him and smiled and said, "That's why we are here, I already ask her father about it, and he said yes, I am your father and I know what is best for you".

Suddenly the wooden drum rang, it was like a storm pounding the heart of Ngongosila, a call for the gathering for the feast, all people great and small answered to the call. The village square was covered with people from different tribes, all here to be part of the great feast, all the food was set before them, Lamawa's father stood up and screamed at the top of his lungs, "let the feast begin".

Everyone was enjoying themselves, people were laughing, telling stories, and eating. Whilst everyone was busy eating, Lamawa's father, Chief Maela, stood up and said, he wanted to make a declaration to all his kin and tribesmen. "I wish to declare my daughter Lamawa, the great explorer will be married to Oge, the son of chief Luda from Kwai Island".

There was a big silence for a moment, then suddenly everyone started jumping and screaming in celebration, because this union would mean even more, these two tribes will now become one because of the marriage, they will all become one people.

After the announcement, Oge's father stood up and laid out twenty shell money and four pigs and said now Lamawa will be my son's wife, from now on she will be under my care, I will take full responsibility as she is my own child. This feast is not only a symbol of our harvest month but also a new beginning, a new dawn for the people of Kwai and Ngongosila, now my people will be your people, my land will be your land.

That same evening Lamawa was taken to the hut where the people of Kwai lived, Kini and a few women from Kwai brought her into the hut and she spent the night there.

The next day it was time for them to leave for Kwai Islands. All the warriors were preparing the canoes for the long journey ahead, they stocked up their canoes with food and water and were then ready to go.

Chief Maela come to say his last goodbye to his daughter, with tears in his eyes, he said, "come back to me when you have your first child so I can bless him". They shook hands and bid farewell to each other.

Oge and his new wife Lamawa were in their own canoe, the people from Kwai set sail out into the open sea, setting their course straight to Kwai Island, it was a bit windy that day, so it was a good ride back home for the sailors, they were singing and celebrating on their journey home.

Chief Maela was standing on the beach looking towards the setting sun until, the party disappear into the sun.

Oge and Lamawa lived on and have a beautiful family, the legend of the great explorer lived on, and how the two tribes become one. There were many more trips and feasts between the two Islands, chief Maela, did finally meet the first-born son of Oge and Lamawa before he died. He was able to bless his grandson and given him the name of his great grandfather Tiba.

Lamawa did have three more sons after, which she named one of them after his late father. They lived happily ever after, Lamawa was a great woman, and he teaches his sons about the way of the sea.

The sons grew up to become great men of the people of Kwai, they lived their own lives and have their own stories, because of the knowledge they learn from their mother, they do much more exploration outside of Kwai and Ngongosila and discovered a few other islands.

Oge and Lamawa grew old together, their love for each other never stops, they spend each and every moment together. They live life to the fullest, Oge become Chief after his late father and his son will be after him, he led with great knowledge and wisdom. Lamawa became his counsel in matters that he could not handle alone.

In the end life still goes on, generations come and go. People will come and go like the waves hitting the shores of the coastline, but our names will live on forever, strangers will tell our stories, the things we do now will become myths and legends. It was believed that Lamawa was the only one who knew the path that leads to the secret garden, she did not tell her sons about it, she took those secrets with her to the grave. Lamawa died at a very old age, not alone but with her sons and grandchildren beside her, living in this world with a complete fulfilled life.

◊ **Leleko fish:** A type of fish that is very special to island people, during the season once you eat it you will have bad dreams.
◊ **Gwabi:** A traditional type of way to cook food in an open fire oven

The End

Acknowledgements

Writing *"A Girl from Kwai and Ngongosila"* has been an incredible journey, and I am deeply grateful to all who have supported and inspired me along the way.

First and foremost, I want to express my heartfelt gratitude to my family for their unwavering support and encouragement. Your belief in me has been my greatest motivation.

To my friends and colleagues, thank you for your valuable feedback and for always being there to listen and offer advice. Your insights have been invaluable in shaping this story.

I am also deeply appreciative of the rich cultural heritage of Kwai and Ngongosila, which provided the backdrop for this story. The vibrant traditions and stories of the people have been a wellspring of inspiration.

Special thanks to the First Nations Writers Team for this great opportunity and being part of it. Your expertise and encouragement have been instrumental in bringing this story to life.

Lastly, I want to thank all the readers who have taken the time to read and engage with this story. Your interest and feedback are greatly appreciated and encourage me to continue writing. Thank you all for being a part of this journey.

Geena Iga Kuson

Of Papua New Guinea

The Judges

The Judges said " A wonderful story, and common everywhere in the world. However here it is filled with the culture of the village and the city, of family and neighbours, and the heartache of a broken family. Of tenacity and loss and survival. And the future."

This story is so humble and so gently spoken, that we may miss the deeper meanings of loss at a young age, of not only immediate family, but also opportunities, of stability and of enriching relationships that are intended to hold you close from birth, to build you up.

Then it reaches out and illustrates, that with obstinate perseverance and audacity, and extended family, these challenges or "losses" are able to be converted to creating the person you become, and provide for all the structures you missed. So, you emerge stronger, indeed, maybe even better.

Many lessons here, wonderfully told.

Ravu Mo, Sail On

Geena Iga Kuson

Chapter 1: The Call

My father called the other day, breaking the years of silence that separated us. His voice, a blend of weariness and desperation, cut through the airwaves. I suspected it would be his voice and regretted answering the call but it was too late.

"Gina!" he asked with certainty, "Yes", I humbly replied. "Me laikim sampla coins lo busfare go bek ken lo peles" he uttered. As his custom was, he begins by asking for the kind of support only a father could seek. He needed money to return home after visiting his nephew, a victim of a sudden stroke.

For years, his absence had been a prevailing theme in the story of my life. His journey was a shadowed one, veiled from my understanding. The prayers I offered for him were more wishes for peace, health, and faith, not for a connection to be rekindled.

As I pondered his request, memories flooded my mind like a dam bursting forth. His face, a distant visage from the past, carried the weight of neglect. My upbringing was void of his presence, my childhood a canvas painted without his brushstrokes. My mother, a silent heroine, had borne the burden of raising me alone, working tirelessly to ensure my well-being. Anger bubbled within me, a tempest waiting to unleash its fury. The temptation to unveil the painful past and seek revenge was deep. My bones, hardened by the touch of my mother's calloused hands, ached for justice. Yet, where I come from, revenge is not the answer.

I was born and raised in a special place by special people of Irupara Village. The blood and grace of my people has molded me with integrity, love, respect and humility toward my enemy.

Chapter 2: Heading home

The door of the room slammed hard, I could hear my dad shout with all his strength, his nerve-wrecking voice vibrated and echoed down the ladder ahead of his footsteps. His steps moved swiftly and the whole house shook with his fury.

Dad and Mum oftener argued recklessly, screaming with anger and pain so loud our neighbors could hear all they were saying. Most times I shy away and tuck myself in a corner of the house watching all the drama that unfolds. Frequently, after the quarrel, dad would leave. I could see the pain of being alone in my mother's eyes when he left. And when dad leaves, he never returns home until after two weeks and at times after a month.

As a child I wondered why the arguments were so heated with an outcome of such repellent effect. Mum and I used to be alone at home. Dad always had his relatives live with us so when he leaves, his relatives still remain at home. It was a difficult challenge for mum to show kindness to them. But with me, she had one who could live with her through her tough times and I knew the burden was lighter with my presence.

These were trying times for her as a new mum; she held onto her faith and drew strength from her prayers. She had learnt to stay in tune with her faith for she had been taught well to trust in the Lord in life's darkest moment. She was blessed with the climax of a youthful life, a home and a new family - one could anticipate; she was just twenty-five years old when I was born. A perfect time to live up to her dreams and goals she had in life.

However, this was inevitable, the ongoing quarrels were a bad tumor, eating her up gradually inside, she couldn't take it any longer. Her best judgment was to send me home to her parents knowing full well her daughter will be looked after with good care. She thought that it was best for her to walk this road alone and that I should not have an unfortunate upbringing.

So, with a heavy heart, she neatly packed my clothes into a bag, with tears streaming down her cheeks, she prayed for the decision she was making. She hid her emotions and cried bitterly while I was playing.

The day soon arrived, she got me to sit down on the bed, the orange hues of the sun peered through the windows, the room filled with the coolness of the afternoon. Mum began to explain clearly her approach of sending me home so that I could understand. It felt miserable but I understood bitterly the situation between mum and dad. I knew my attachment toward dad will slowly fade knowing I won't be around him often but I had to accept my mother's decision hoping things would get better.

Very early the next morning, mum and I showered. I got into the change of clothes she neatly placed on the edge of the bed, long jeans and a white round neck. She instructed me to carry a lighter bag while she carried my bag which was heavier. We grabbed the bags and walked out of the house.

My father's relatives, who remained at home, had no say in my mother's decision and raised their hands to wave me their goodbye. I was anxious and filled with mixed emotions. Leaving home to be with my grandparents was something else.

I anticipated heading to the village as it was adventurous knowing the company of my cousins. And I remained calm to my mother's lead. We walked out to the bus stop and hopped on a bus numbered four (4), which took the route from Konedobu through Koki and then to Gordons. We arrived at Kina Mart, Waigani.

Kina Mart was where all the PMV trucks from Rigo coast came to a stop and picked up passengers to head to the village. I was excited, we secured the seats in a PMV truck, purchased some basic food like rice and flour, basic detergents and some junk to munch on in the PMV.

We were on the highway two hundred of Central Province, heading for the Magi Highway toward Irupara Village. As we passed the valley filled with humongous elephant grass, the mountains stood tall with firm structure, the green pine trees filled the mountains while the blue sea lay beautifully calm, I forgot the longing of my father. I was heading home as was destined.

Chapter 3: Adapting to the village life

Mum was a nursing officer and had a full-time job at the General Hospital in Port Moresby, so she had to return the next day. When mum got picked up early around 4am the next day, I cried bitterly missing her presence. "Mummy!" I cried loudly and sat on the veranda seeing the PMV drive off until its lights faded and the sound of the truck couldn't be heard in the distance.

I ran into the mosquito net and wept quietly afraid my grandfather might scold me for crying too much. I slept on my wet pillow and dried my eyes with the blanket around me. In my little mind, I knew this was best for mum and I had to make it easier for her to get into good terms with dad. I had to put up with the village life.

It wouldn't be too easy and I depended on my grandmother's teaching and mum's elderly sister, Aunty Grace. Aunt Grace was adorable, humble and caring and I found peace leaning into her when mum wasn't around. My cousins were always around to cheer me with their stories and their playful tactics. I was glad to have my cousins, Paul, Solomon and Junior, who was a complete dramatic lunatic. They were not only my play mates but my best of friends. They embraced me with their companionship and gave me a place of belonging.

This replaced the feeling from the absence of my parents. I observed and quicky picked up the daily routine of how they lived in the village. When grandfather planned to go fishing, we (the children) were tasked to assist him to the beach, push his hand-made canoe off the coast and into the sea, then ensured he packed all his fishing gear onto the canoe.

We would stand gazing out to sea and admired him for venturing off into the sea, paddling his way out further and further. The waves splashed against the canoe and when he felt that he was good to go he would then instruct us to go home. "Bye bubu" was our usual response. We waved him goodbye and playfully ran home abiding by his instructions.

By sunset, we returned to the sea to wait for his return. We played and watched the sunset, keeping a lookout to see if grandfather was paddling back. It was always a vivid moment paddling toward the village from the ocean. The sun would gradually sink behind him leaving an orange and pink horizon in the clear sky, with a distant shadow of his figure on the canoe.

Our hearts leapt when learning of his return. We anticipated fish for dinner. Sometimes it was a good catch; other times, he returned home with no single catch and we would share the sentiment of his effort by saying "sorry, bubu". But when grandfather returned with the abundance of reef fish, we leaped with joy.

Our smiling faces followed the instructions of grandfather to collect the fish and put them into the bags. The best and the biggest fish was always given to the tithe house. A symbol of his faith in returning the best to the Lord.

Other fish would be shared to many families and we would gladly adhere to his instruction of carrying a string of fish to his siblings and their family. Enough was brought home for dinner. We enjoyed a delicious soup of creamed fish and garden food.

When grandmother and aunt planned to go gardening, we were all tasked to follow them carrying a hoe, a knife, a spade or a bag. Instructions were usually given before we walked toward the garden, then a prayer was usually ascended for protection. These chores were a delight as we did them together.

Apart from gardening we collected water from the well about twenty meters from the house. The well was isolated and fetching water wasn't just a chore; it was a ritual that allowed my mind to wander into the realms of the future.

As the pail dipped into the well and water sloshed into the buckets, my thoughts pondered the struggles and challenges that led me home. It was during these moments, with the weight of water in my hands, that I contemplated my dreams in life. The steps, back and forth with buckets in hand, laid the path towards self-discovery. The burden of those buckets taught me to be strong, to strive, to endure, and to grow beyond the confines of poverty and without parents there and then. With each journey to the well, my confidence grew, and I started making choices that would shape my destiny.

Today, as I return home for the holidays, I find those buckets of water nearly impossible to lift. My bare hands, once accustomed to the weight, now struggle under the burden. Yet, these buckets of water, once heavy and bulky, have propelled me to this point. They were more than vessels for water; they were vessels of determination and resilience, paving the way for a life beyond the limitations of my beginnings.

In the quiet moments spent carrying water, I learned that life's burdens, like buckets filled to the brim, can be heavy. But it's the strength we gain from carrying them that shapes our journey. Those buckets of water, once a symbol of struggle, are now a testament to the path I've traveled—a journey of growth, perseverance, and the transformation of challenges into stepping stones toward a brighter future.

Days turned into months and I soon forgot about my parent's marital issue. I was living the best time of my life with mum's sister, her children and my grandparents. They were now my family.

Chapter 4: Getting things right

Of all the time we had together and functioned as a family, there was a special moment that knitted us as a family. This bond has been embedded in our hearts and will always be there until we rest in the grave of which the Lord calls.

Grandfather always had this special way of calling for worship, "Oe oe oe!".

This was a signal of the time for family worship. We spent time together listening to the stories of the bible and found courage in the stories shared. We spent time together before sun rise and when the sun set. It was a call to commit our plans and daily tasks to the Lord and be thankful at the end of a day of the blessings enjoyed during the day. We would be encouraged by a verse from the Morning Watch list in the morning and then a Bible Reading in the evening. Prayer was always consistent.

This was where we drew our strength, lived our hope and were inspired to live meaningfully in the ordinary moments of our life in the village. The indomitable spirit of my grandfather still lives in our lives today and I am forever grateful to have learned this special ingredient of life as a child.

On Friday's we were encouraged to clean the house early during the day and cook food before three in the afternoon. We were to prepare early for Sabbath. We would grill the long tom fish over the fire and help the mothers to scrape coconut, peel the garden food and make a fire.

Tapioca, was a staple food that we place in a huge aluminum pot with extremely hot stones heated with fire. Saturday was known as Sabbath and always a day off as we rested from all our chores and the activities that we did for six days. We attended church and extra curricula activities the church organised, the whole day.

Worship was the center of this program. Naturally, as children we always wanted to play but couldn't on this day. Our grandparents honoured the day by going to church and sharing the daily encounter with God. Though we looked forward for the sun to go down quickly as playing always got the best of us and we often got scolded when we ignorantly played and when we did not keep quiet. My grandparents always reminded us with the words from the scriptures in Exodus 20: 8, Remember the Sabbath Day to keep it Holy.

Worship was and is the central part of our life in the village, apart from gardening, fishing and community work. The Christian faith was my people's way of getting things right, rising to the crucibles of a home and outliving the unfortunate circumstance.

I thought my answer was right there and then. And little did I realise God had prepared me as a child to be resilient and to outlive the unforeseen circumstances of my family background to live upright with future endeavors. I have learnt to get things done the right way and interestingly this, I held dearly as solution to challenges while growing.

Chapter 5: My family

The days of longing for my parents finally kicked in. I missed mum a little too much and though I tried to be strong, the sad emotion overwhelmed my fears and I hoped for the best of her with dad. I quietly cried to sleep at night thinking of her and feeling how I missed her. I knew I had to hear from her sooner or later.

So, I asked my aunt, "Aunty, is mum ever going to come for a weekend?" "I do not know that, Gina, but we'll send word for her and find out" she responded.

I trusted aunty and settled with her response. She assured me that she would find out. It was in mid-1995, six months have passed from the last time I saw her. I wondered if she was okay, I wondered how dad might have been toward her. My imaginations ran wild which brought tears to my littles eyes. I was only six years old and had learnt to be independent at a very young age. When the PMV trucks arrived from town on a week day and ran past our home to drop other passengers, I sometimes wished it stopped to drop mum. I wished one day mum would arrive just as how she had come to leave me. My little heart dropped when there was no sigh so I turned to wander off and play.

Nevertheless, mum shops and send's our ration each fortnight. We call it "Ugukau". Our staple food was rice and flour and we received it from the PMV trucks that brought them safely. In this way, I felt connected to her despite her absence. We shared the food and all ate together.

I later learned that dad had another family. This was the reason why he always left us to be with his new family. The arguments were a scapegoat so that that he could be with them.

Mum was a heroine and forever my inspiration who stood firm in her role as a mother and never gave up her job. She cared for the sick so I could have a life. Dad was back home with her but unstable. I can vividly remember countless appearances in the courthouse when mum opted to legally sort their marital issues. Sad to say, dad somehow maneuvers and slip through the Judge.

Life was interesting knowing about his other family which makes them mine too. I hesitantly accept such reality as I was content and ever happy to be with my grandparents, my aunt and her children. It wasn't a perfect one, but we shared a special bond of trust and caring for each other. I never wanted to be elsewhere as this was my safe haven.

Chapter 6: A new chapter

My small brother was born the next year. A huge round black baby with strong hair like an African. I had no idea whether mum and dad where now together but the birth of my small brother had given me hope. Life took on its toll as mum continued to sustain us both. This time, Jeremy whom my small aunt named, was now part and parcel of the same challenge.

Having a small brother made me feel obliged to support mum in any way possible. Feeding the baby, caring for him while mum did laundry, or at times replacing the nappies was an interesting chore. I'd like to think that where else could we learn to be mothers in the future but our very home.

Many times, I got carried away playing with my cousins while her sisters met the emotional and physical support. Mum's sisters offered to help mum babysit while she juggled work. And especially Aunty Grace came in to support full time. She had her share of problems and had five children to care for; nevertheless, she cared for us like her own when mum was in her marital crisis.

As I reflect, we are forever grateful for all her love and sacrifice. Her love for her sister has been one that we adore and we'll carry in our hearts. This has been a testament of healing in my life. Little did I realise her love and support has neutralised the absence of a father in my life.

My small brother and I are six years different in age, so grew apart with our own interests. Life has been the same, dad continued to be a womaniser while mum remained content with us, her children.

In the year 2002, mum got tired of his attitude and retired home. With her retirement benefits, she contributed to buy housing materials. She had asked of her father to make an extension to the family house downstairs. So, we had a place to stay.

My father had joined her in the quest to live in the village. This was an interesting move but I was happy that I would have him forever by my side. He was from a different land and I felt sad that he had to adapt to the way we live and do things in the village. I knew my presence would ease his challenges and so I did try to be around him so he could be comfortable. My grandparents embraced him despite his background and I strongly believed had him in his prayers.

After a year, mum saw life was a great challenge at home. In her retirement, she had built a home and bought huge coolers to use to store fresh fish to resell. When there was a good catch by the divers, she would buy from them and bring them to town early the next day to resell. This was not an easy task, she struggled to make ends meet.

So, she decided to apply for jobs. She had secured a position at the Hula Sub Health Centre. This means we were going back to where she began work, a little distance further from our village. This was special to me because mum had given birth to me in this smaller cubical ward of twenty-five square meters. We looked forward to a new environment but felt a longing to remain with my grandparents.

Mum was glad that she would work and could earn a little extra so that we could have some sort of financial support. We finally moved up to Hula Village. There was a room for myself and my parents, who had a bigger one. After cleaning the new house, we finally moved up.

We packed our cargo on the dingy we had asked to help. Off the dingy slowly drifted out as it was filled with mattress and bags. When the skipper steered onto the deep, he steered in the direction. The front of the dingy lifted its head as sides broke through the waves and headed straight to hood point. Our house was a minute walk in from the sea and so we arrived within fifteen minutes.

We carried all the cargo out of the dingy and straight to the house. It was a fun and I enjoyed it. The house had a well of fresh water, a structured shower and a sheltered kitchen. This was more appropriate. Our neighbors were kind people from Koiari.

The house we were in had a small room downstairs which accommodated the cleaner of the campus. I finally settled in my own room. At night the breeze blew from the sea, the waves crashed on the coast and we slept a peaceful night. It was a wonderful treat from the challenges we endured financially from the past years.

The clinic was a minute's walk. Mum went to work close by while I commuted to and from the primary school inland.

Dad was also with us through this transition as was my smaller brother who was ready to attend the elementary school nearby.

With this new chapter of our journey, mum now was expecting a third child. Through her pregnancy, she enjoyed serving people, caring for the sick and the needy and she did not waiver from her faith and her profession. Hula Sub Health Centre was a church run clinic under the United Church Diocese. It accommodated four nursing officers and a sister in charge.

Though mum and her colleagues were not fully paid at times, she never gave up serving. Sometimes their pay was delayed, at times it was postponed another fortnight to get double. These we did not foresee but, believed that God had made providences through our neighbors, and friends and people who shared food when we needed it.

Mum was a great help to many and so her kindness was repaid in surprising ways. Dad was also an outspoken person and easily socialised with the locals. He made new friends and had close buddies that went diving and shared with him fish for dinner.

Chapter 7: Sail On

Dad started spending time with his friends more than his family. It became a concern when dad was not at home most nights or came home late. We knew he was with his friends. But it became a continuous practice and so unusual that mum became suspicious of his moves.

We later found out dad was seeing a local woman who lived a distance from the clinic. This was a frustrating episode.

Someone told mum where they had seen dad with another women. Mum had been expecting a third child. She was deeply hurt and imagined breaking my father's head with a stone.

She kept this news to herself and never wanted to tell me. I could tell something was not right when she scolded dad each time he returned home in the early hours of the morning.

One day, mum was cleaning the room and wanted to do laundry so she separated clothes to wash and found on dad's dirty shirt a thread of a single loose hair. It didn't match our strong hair.

Since then, mum has confirmed the story of her husband sleeping with the native lady. Mums' reputation and pride for quality nursing service had been deprived. She was stressed from this kind of life. She thought, heading home was a way out from this kind of life, however dad never ceased his habit of womanising. Mum was pregnant at eight months and was suffering from appendicitis.

One evening, dad went out as usual and didn't come home. Mothers' appendicitis was painful and hurt so bad she couldn't sleep. It was around three in the morning. We sent word to Mr. Koivi, mother's colleague who lived next to us, to alert the ambulance to rush her into town – The Port Moresby General Hospital.

The pain was excruciating. I was in grade seven, matured to understand what was happening. I helped mum quickly pack her bag of clothes and the babies' clothes in case she would go through surgery. While doing so mum gave me careful instructions to adhere to. I listened carefully and noted what to do when she left.

Jeremy and I stood in the living room and watched through the screen. The lights of the ambulance faded in the distance as it sped off. We cried bitterly not knowing what will become of her. We went back to her room and lay quietly with hope burning in our hearts that she would be better. Prayer was the only thing we knew. There was nothing we could do but bring our agenda to God in prayer. Jeremy and I closed our eyes for a short prayer and laid our heads to sleep. We finally slept knowing the sun would rise in no time.

When the rays of the sun swept through the screen of the window, it heated our faces and we both leapt simultaneously with exhaustion and gathered ourselves. My small brother and I walked along the beach to Irupara to advise grandfather and aunt of the incident, that was my mother's instruction. It was low tide and we crossed over the river with the sea on our knees. We have learnt to be courageous at a young age and fend for each other.

Dad had arrived in the morning but there was nothing he could do. He looked for a PMV and headed down to check on mother.

One afternoon, in the same week, Aunty Gwen, mother's colleague who had been closely monitoring her progress in Port Moresby notified me as I was heading back from school, she said "Gina, mum had given birth to a baby girl". I smiled with joy to know mum was fine with child. I wasn't sure which gender would perfectly be acceptable and I could say no more.

Mother later shared that her appendicitis had burst while in the village and the doctors had to remove it. It was healthier to remove the child as well. That was how we had a baby sister earlier than expected.

Unfortunately, dad had left us at this time to be with his partner for the rest of his life. We were now on our own. This time, mum made a firm decision not to entertain him nor accept him back into her life anymore. My father had left to create a new family of his own at the birth of the third child. Mum made her final decision and stood by it. When dad attempted to visit her at the hospital, she never bothered to buy into his caring deeds. It hurt so badly to live this kind of life through with a man who continues to live his life in lustful ways.

My baby sister grew without the presence of a father. She was born on the 30th of November, 2002. A beacon in our most trying time.

Dad finally left. We were alone but free. There wouldn't be much of stress with his life. We had to fend for ourselves and survive life's pressing challenges on our own. We have learnt to be resilient; we knew our faith in God was a special ingredient to overcome life's challenges that came our way. We were happy with mum by our side as she was our strong tower. Mother was a stronghold as she picked up the broken pieces of our life and sailed on with three on board.

The End

Acknowledgements

To my late grandparents, Pr. Wala Iga and Mrs. Martha Wala, who gave me life at its best and taught me to be resilient and stand by faith and Godly principles in life's darkest moments. My aunt, Grace Wala and children, Paul and Solomon who gave me in their heart a place to belong. Your loving acts of kindness has not shifted away with time unnoticed. Junior Kenneth

Milton, my cousin, who had me cheering and laughing in my lowest point of life with your endless dramas. To my mum, Mrs. June Wala Wolly whose life is my inspiration, the reason why I keep writing.

Kogora Hale
Of Papua New Guinea

The Judges

The Judges said "A seemingly simple story however one filled with joy, and cultural observations that remind readers of village life and customs. Another elegant story from Mr Hale."

His stories are inherently clever for their simplicity in sharing life, hopes and dreams of growing up in a PNG village. They may be read lightly or deeply, which is a very difficult style to master. Mr Hale has mastered this style in spades.

Measurements and Patterns

Kogora Hale

Andrew passed the third store. He recognised the storekeeper, a friend of one of Hane's brothers. He waved but the boy didn't wave back, instead he fixed his glasses on his small round face and turned away.

Andrew thought the boy looked like Ranpo Edogwa from Bungou Stray dogs. Perhaps like Ranpo the detective, he could see right through Andrew's emptiness.

Andrew picked up his pace, amused at his own thoughts. It was a little past nine when he left home a short while ago. The road to Hane's place wasn't far. A 30 minute walk across the middle of the village and then up a short hilly terrain, then through a grove of mango trees. Hane's home was in a secluded area, away from the main village, with few other homes further inland.

All these houses had only Ranpo's store to visit, Andrew noted. He was a skilled sewist. Part of his daily task included taking measurements; that included counting. Counting had become part of him, like singing. But the latter he seldom did, having accepted the sad reality that his voice was much like a frog's. But counting happened in your head. So he loved it. He had counted three stores since taking this road. One of them was closed with a big board across the counter, testament to the owner's mismanagement. Seven roadside market stalls, all filled with hardworking pretty girls, but none as striking as his Hane. Then there were eight stray dogs, two were in critical condition. Hunger had turned them into walking skeletons. Andrew sighed and turned away, behind him he could hear one of the dog's yelping in pain.

Apart from a chocolate in his bilum, he had nothing on him. He couldn't afford a drink for himself, nor could he remember all the talk he had practiced while roaming in the woods. Poor Andrew, he had prepared for days, even wrote down two pages of what best to say. But all of that was gone now. His throat felt dry, and the idea of heading back home became more appealing. He could envision the stream behind his home; the slow flow of water, the green stalks he thought of cooking – just to find out if they were edible, the boulders that were twice as big as himself: truly that was an ideal haven for a weary soul like him. But going back now would prove he was a weakling. And he wasn't. No. Andrew was no weakling.

The iron gate to his destination looked uninviting, unwelcoming, even dangerous. Two coconut trees by the side of the gate looked like big Roman whips about to deal with him. He had seen that whip in Gibson's film *The Passion of the Christ* in the village square. How the Roman soldiers beat the Son of God. It was awful. No film had ever brought him to tears like that film.

Two things happened that night; he was more a Christian than he ever was, professing his faith again and vowing to be more faithful. The second thing he noticed was Hane. Her hair glowing under the moonlight, and her chuckle more mysterious than before. He was sure she carried the scent of the Mairava mango. Like the mango season, the thought of her dominated his mind. He was not only certain he was a saved sinner turned saint; he was a saint that needed his Eve.

But unlike the story of Eve, he had to go and talk to her. Like every other village girl, Andrew knew them all. They all grew up together, played together, fought with each other. Had each other's parents stick them. Hane included. But this night Andrew didn't just see Hane. He noticed her.

So, he did the unthinkable. He offered to escort her home afterward. It wasn't like she needed escorting. But she said yes anyway, with eyes as wide as the moon in the sky. You say yes after watching Jim Caviezel's terrific acting, even your brothers will tolerate a convicted friend for a while. Andrew never asked her out or anything, but whatever kindled that fateful night blossomed into something romantic, something true and tried.

And today he was on his way to ask her family for her hand. That was the plan. He wouldn't do what Martin and Shala did; impregnate their girlfriends and then convince their family to have them married. That was sinful of a Christian, and he wasn't going to be a sinner.

The bitter truth was that part of him wanted to disappear from here, another part urged him on. His heart was like when the river meets the sea, and the rendezvous was a heavy commotion in bad weather. It was noisy, far from tranquil.

Andrew had worn a plain blue t-shirt and his worn-out blue jeans. The only jeans he owned and the only wear he hated to wash. But he loved it because he could wear it for a week without washing it. Among his many caps Andrew chose the green one, an army cap. He had different caps for different occasions. He had taken the army one, believing it would instill a sense of someone in control. And it did; he felt like someone in control, that is until he turned a corner and was face-to-face with the familiar iron gate. He had never gone beyond that gate. In a swift move he pulled off his army cap and swung it into his bilum.

'You can do this,' Andrew whispered under his breath.

He pushed open the gate and stepped in.

Hane had prepared a light meal for her family on their verandah. She made it seem like her boyfriend had bought everything. The truth was they both received help from a lady that need not be known now. She had thrown a sago mat on the floor, carried out some chairs, and dressed a short knee-high table with colorful material. It was one of Andrew's many gifts to her. She straightened the edges, placed cups and a container of orange juice on it.

She offered a smile to Tau, who was also helping with the chairs. He disappeared again and came out with a tray of baked bread. His friends had left him for the forest a while ago. Tau was upset he would be missing such a trip. What kind of gathering was this that needed all the family members present? He did hide his scowl from Hane and his father. He was sure it had something to do with Andrew; that ostrich with long legs.

The three brothers each sat on a chair, except for Tobi, the youngest, who was already a prey to Andrew's attempts for kinship. He sat on his mother's lap on the floor, occasionally fiddling with his father's couch; a couch that had undergone a thorough renovation to suit Mr. Matavai's lofty notions of family headship. Mr. Matavai had both his sons, Mike and Tau, fix the couch for him. They had removed the curtain in the living room and covered the couch, giving it a fresh look.

The two brothers each disliked Andrew for different reasons. Mike believed Andrew was too long and too weak, and didn't speak like a native. His Gado, their local language, was polluted; mixed with some English and the next village's dialect. He was not a true Henanuan.

As for Tau, he hated Andrew the first time he saw him hold Hane's hand. That was years ago at the village square after a movie night. But Tau never forgave him, nor did he succeed in having his small gang belt the boy up. They had planned to have him eat chilly afterward, and then throw him in his own river. If Andrew succeeded in swimming to safety, then heaven agreed that he was good for his sister.

But Tau never achieved his evil scheme. Vaika, the older brother, loved his sister and was willing to see her heart's desire granted. He acted nonchalant before his father, arms and legs crossed. He had contributed, with the other anonymous lady, towards this little meeting. Hane was so happy she personally carried Vaika's chair out. Vaika had shut down today's business runs to be present in this meeting.

The family had pulled a long chord out with Mr. Matavai's fan to counter the heat. Tau had locked all the dogs away, he didn't want them sniffing about like he didn't feed them. Not when someone like Andrew was coming up.

'Here he comes,' Tobi shouted. He grasped at his mother playfully before a harsh rebuke put him in his place. 'But it's Andrew, Mama. He always gives me -.' 'Hush, quiet,' Mrs. Matavai said, 'you behave or I'll send you off.'

'Bring him up,' Mrs. Matavai told Hane, who quickly skipped down the steps to meet Andrew. When they came up everyone was a bit surprised to see Andrew's shirt drenched in sweat. No one said anything, and Andrew was happy that Hane slid a cold cup of juice into his hands. Everyone waited as he drank his juice. Andrew wisely took his time, each gulp enough to buy him time to recall his early morning meditations. But his mind turned up blank, like a board wiped of chalk. He was startled when he realized the cup was already empty.

'I'm sorry,' he mumbled.

'Do not worry,' Mr. Matavai answered, motioning with his hand for a chair. Mike pushed a chair with his foot toward Andrew. 'Take, sit.'

'Your house is beautiful,' Andrew said nervously. He looked from Tobi's beaming face to other more frightening faces. Some expressionless.

'I hear you live at Kanai,' Mrs. Matavai said. 'With the dry season like this, is the river dried up already?' No, the river is not dry. It has never been dry before, Andrew explained. 'Once upon a time before I was born, my mom said it nearly dried. Just when it was to go dry, a heavy rain fell and everything came back to normal.' Andrew stopped. No one was here to hear his story about the river. He put the cup back on the table and looked at Mr. Matavai with the most loving smile he could muster. It was only proper the man lead the talk. But the guy simply busied himself with pouring another juice.

The verandah was larger up close. Andrew always imagined the verandah to be big, but not this spacious. He noticed the windows had no louver and curtains. Someone drew a monkey's face on the wall with a name: Tobi. An orange flower pot hung from the roof, its leaf reminding him of the stalks he was yet to cook at the river.

~

'You have a nice bilum,' Tau said.

Mike nodded in agreement. 'I bet you just borrowed it today. I mean most people do that, right? They wear their aunt's bilum just to appear more …'More stylish,' Tau said. 'Some even go next-door to borrow bilums. We are not -.'

'Andrew actually sows his own bilums,' Hane interjected, beaming with a smile. 'Tell them, Andrew.'

'I do, yes,' Andrew said. He passed his bilum to the boys to inspect. 'It's not hard. Sewing a bilum is all about measurements and patterns. You memorise patterns and then just repeat them. That's it.'

The two boys watched. If they were interested, they didn't show it. They passed it to their mom, then to their father, who only nodded. 'This is excellent, actually,' Mrs. Matavai said. 'He has employed a style even woman my age are yet to master.'

'So is that all you can do? Make bilum?' Mike asked.

'I thought sewing was for women?' Tau added.

'Who in the world said that?' Vaika said. He had been quiet enough. 'Sewing is a skill. You have better chances of surviving in this country if you have such skills. Have you seen graduates looking for jobs in the city? It's heart breaking. You two should learn something like that or dad and mom will forever feed you.'

'But it's different,' Mike complained. 'This boy is just here to take our sister.'

'That's enough,' Mr. Matavai said. His voice carried authority, like thunder it slit through the brewing commotion. 'Tau, you and Mike leave quietly. Now.' The two boys left, but head held high, locking gaze with their visitor till they passed into their living room.

'So Hane tells me you have something to say today,' Mr. Matavai said. He folded his arms and reclined on his chair, his face fixed on the young man. He had had his own ideas about what this gathering was about. It wasn't hard to tell. Hane had been a good girl for like a month before telling her dad that an Andrew wanted to see him. She had been making his favorite soup for a week, ensured that his cigar never ran out, or that sugar and tea bags never ran low. Matavai loved drinking tea, and had deciphered his daughter's cunning tricks a long time ago.

Andrew had pulled a chocolate from his bilum and handed it to Toby. He felt better not having to deal with the two brothers. Andrew wished Hane would have sat beside him. He thought that was the sensible thing to do.

'Will you make an old man wait this long? Mr. Matavai shifted uncomfortably.

'Yes, yes, forgive me,' Andrew said. He waited for his lungs to become full with air. 'I am here to ask if I can marry your daughter, Sir.' When Mr. Matavai took a while to answer he added, 'I think as a man I might not tick off all your ideals of a good husband, but Sir I love your daughter and I will do anything to see her well.'

'Mhh,' Mr. Matavai grunted. 'Young people and marriage.'

'But Sir, I'm not young, I'm 23.'

'23 is young, boy.'

'Sir, my father got married when he was 17,' Andrew said.

'You are not your father, and I am not your mother's father.'

'But I will look after your daughter very well, Sir.'

'I have not even said yes yet, boy.'

Mrs. Matavai felt she would burst into laughter any moment. Her husband wasn't high and mighty like this when he almost crawled to her father's house 31 years ago. She imagined tossing that story on the table now and seeing the reaction from everyone. Little Toby had exited with his chocolate. He understood little of the event that was unfolding. All he knew was that Andrew had for the first time come right home to see Hane. After this he would be allowed to come home, or even stay for dinner. That meant only one good thing: more chocolates. Mrs. Matavai poured juice and passed the bread around. Andrew appreciated the short break.

'Do you live with your parents?' Mr. Matavai asked.

'Yes, Sir,' Andrew nodded.

'So they still look after you then.'

'My parents are much older than you, Sir. I look after them. My siblings have all married and left.'

'Why didn't you bring your parents?' Mrs. Matavai said.

Andrew hesitated again. He looked from Vaika to Hane, hoping the sight of her would strengthen him. 'My mom wants me to marry another girl.'

Mrs. Matavai raised her brows, 'And?'

'I have eyes only for your daughter.'

'I like this boy,' Vaika laughed. 'And who's this other girl?'

'My mom's friend's daughter. They say she's more a village girl than Hane.'

'And what do you say of Hane?'

Andrew had been staring at the floor. He looked up at Vaika. Words got stuck in his throat like fish bone. 'I love Hane. She is the only thing that makes sense to me.'

'Love won't feed anybody,' Mr Matavai said. 'Tell me, do you have your own garden?'

Andrew had three gardens, he told them proudly. One was a banana garden, the other a yam garden. The last one was the smallest, a vegetable garden. He was not making this up. Hane had seen them for herself. He hoped to tell the family he already had his sewing business running, with more than twenty clients, most from different villages. But the idea always seemed feminine to him. It was certainly not accepted well among his friends. He didn't want to take his chances with Mr. Matavai. The man appeared to be from the old breed. So he kept this out of his explanation. He noticed Mr. Matavai sat straight when he spoke about the banana garden. 'If I remember correctly, I like four different kinds of bananas growing.'

'Do you have the 2-minute one?'

'Yes, I do. That's my favorite.'

'I haven't eaten those for some time now,' Mr. Matavai admitted, casting an accusing look at his wife.

'That time I brought you ripe bananas,' Hane had found her voice, happy to add to the conversation. 'That was from his garden. Mike and Tau were the ones who ate all of them. Imagine, all of them.'

Andrew couldn't imagine how two stomachs could eat that whole bunch, but he let it pass. He was happy to put Hane's father at peace. The stories he had gathered about the man

weren't true. He wasn't scary, or mean. And no, he didn't kill boys who had big plans for his daughter. Martin and Shala had gone to great lengths trying to dissuade him. They said Hane's father was no mere man. He had influence within the dark community. One wrong word and he'd be buried early. Martin suggested he should find a button phone and record the entire conversation. If he died later on his family would just use the recording as evidence. But Mr. Matavai looked normal enough.

'You seem like a hard working person. I like that. Plus, you came all the way, not many young men would do that.'

Mrs. Matavai nodded with a bright face. She admired the boy's courage, but more than that, she admired him for the fact that he could sew. He was the youngest sewer in the village, the only male sewer, renowned in the nearby villages. But toward this skill of his, he cast little light. No wonder. He spoke of his gardens with all of his heart, but nothing of his sewing skill. Mrs. Matavai believed that the notion that sewing was only for females had gotten to him.

'Why keep the boy waiting,' Vaika said to his father. 'Give him an answer and send him away.'

'Tomorrow morning,' Mr. Matavai said. He couldn't keep his thirst for nicotine at bay any longer. 'I will send my wife to your house. She will give you my answer.'

'Thank you, Sir,' Andrew said. He fumbled for something more to say and ended up grinning like a fool.

'Do you think you can sew a cover for my couch?' Mr. Matavai asked.

'Sew?'

'I hear you are good at it, the sewing stuff.'

'Oh yes,' Andrew said. 'I can always try, Sir.'

Mr. Matavai shook the boy's hands. 'I like that. How come you know sewing?'

'It's just measurements and patterns, Sir. My grandma has a sewing machine. I learnt from her.'

Mr. Matavai nodded and smiled. 'Tomorrow my wife will come see you. You go safely now, Okay?'

'Yes, Sir.'

Mrs. Matavai escorted Andrew to the gate. Hane had remained to clear the verandah. At the gate Andrew stopped and hugged the woman.

'Hane told me you helped contribute some money. Thank you.'

Mrs. Matavai nodded. 'Hane tells me a great deal about you. Is it true? She said you sewed the primary student's graduation gowns last year?'

'Yes, I did. It's not hard. Like I said, it's all measurements and patterns.'

'Measurements and patterns,' Mrs. Matavai said. She brought out a paper from her pocket, then quietly, 'these are measurements of our curtains. Make eight pieces.'

'Eight pieces, okay.'

'My husband talks, but I am the one that makes decisions in the house. Convince me you are good for my daughter.'

Andrew closed the gate behind him. 'I will be waiting with your curtains tomorrow, Aunty. Goodbye.'

Andrew felt lighter than ever. He skipped along the road singing his grandpa's song. He stopped and picked up one of the stray dogs. The dog's fleas didn't matter. He was feeling good. Nothing mattered anymore. Ranpo with his glasses didn't matter. Mike and Tau didn't matter. He greeted whoever he passed on the road, not bothered by the fact that he didn't have enough materials to sew Mrs. Matavai's curtains. Those things will be resolved come sundown. But for now, he must have this moment. He raised the dog in the air and started singing again. 'Measurements and patterns,' he sung. 'Life is all about measurements and patterns.'

The End

BIOS

Marlene Dee Gray Potoura is a teacher/writer/author/publisher. She is from AROB (Autonomous Region of Bougainville). She lives in Port Moresby and is a teacher at the prestigious Paradise College.

Romney Charles Tabara is a part time Author and lives in Port Moresby, Papua New Guinea with his wife and three children. He has self-published several books on Amazon including Children's, Humour and Religious books. He says this is the first official award he has received and he says "I am deeply humbled and honoured by this achievement."

Willy Jnr Fafoi grew up in the small village of Auki, Malaita province, Solomon Islands. Where he spent his childhood developing a deep appreciation for the traditions of his homeland; always drawn to the beauty and power of words. Attended the University of the South Pacific (USP) in Fiji Laucala, and Vanuatu Emalus Law School. He is dedicated to preserving and celebrating the cultural heritage of the Solomon Islands, and strives to bring these vibrant stories to life in prose and verse.

Geena Iga Kuson graduated with a Bachelor of Technical Education from Divine Word University through Don Bosco Technological Institute, was an Electro Technology Trainer in a private organization, and currently serves as a librarian at Pacific

Adventist University Library, Heritage Centre. Passionate about reading a wide range of topics and poetry.

Kogora Hale. studied literature for two years in UPNG. He has always loved storytelling since childhood and sought to express this through short fiction. Much of the craft of writing he learnt from reading books. Currently he works and lives in Narrogin, Western Australia.

Also available

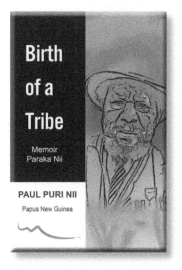

No other private enterprise is publishing
the magnificent stories of
**First Nations peoples of the Greater Pacific.
In the unfiltered voices of the writers.
On a global distribution platform**

We are a registered, regulated, audited Charity, with
Australian Charity and Non-Profit Commission [ACNC]
And DGR tax exempt with the Australian Taxation Office.
All expenses are paid with private bequests and donations.
We have no government support.
All the general workers are unpaid volunteers.
All net funds received through sales are reinvested
in the publications of future stories.

PLEASE DONATE

**In Australia by phone PAYID 79655932979
OR Global on our website
https://firstnationswritersfestival.org/**